"You just haven't woman yet. That look for her."

There were questions in Ripp's eyes; soft needy questions that couldn't be answered entirely with words. Her racing heart screeched almost to a halt as his head slowly dipped toward hers.

"I am looking for her, Lucita," he murmured. "I'm looking right now."

Sensing what was coming, she tried to speak his name, warn him in some way that what he was about to do was fruitless. But nothing would pass her lips.

She could duck her head or jump to her feet and run like a scared rabbit. But those fleeting thoughts didn't stand a chance against the delicious anticipation zipping through her veins. And instead of resisting, something deep within had her leaning toward him, tilting her head so that her lips were totally available to his....

Dear Reader,

Welcome back to the Sandbur ranch!

What a joy it's been for me to write about this branch of
the Ketchum brood. Especially when I can bring a few of
these characters home and remind them how important
it is to be a part of a loving family. As for Lucita, she
believes being back on the Sandbur will turn her and her
son's life in a better direction. Yet neither she, nor any of
her family, can foresee the danger that looms ahead.

Thankfully, there's one tall, lanky deputy sheriff nearby
to protect her. And what a protector he is! Of all the
lawmen I've written about in the past, Ripp McCleod has
snuggled right up to my heart. He's tender, tough and
sexy. And he'll lay his life on the line for Lucita and her
son. What more could a woman ask for?

To all of you readers who've been following my
MEN OF THE WEST series, thank you from the bottom
of my heart. Without you, my writing would mean
nothing and I hope you're as anxious as I am to see
what happens next!

Happy trails!

Stella Bagwell

STELLA BAGWELL

HER TEXAS LAWMAN

Silhouette

SPECIAL EDITION®

Published by Silhouette Books

America's Publisher of Contemporary Romance

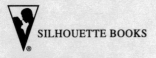 SILHOUETTE BOOKS

ISBN-13: 978-0-373-24911-4
ISBN-10:   0-373-24911-X

HER TEXAS LAWMAN

Copyright © 2008 by Stella Bagwell

STELLA BAGWELL

sold her first book to Silhouette in November 1985. Now, she still loves her job and says she isn't completely content unless she's writing. She and her husband live in Seadrift, Texas, a sleepy little fishing town located on the coastal bend. Stella says the water, the tropical climate and the seabirds make it a lovely place to let her imagination soar and to put the stories in her head down on paper.

She and her husband have one son, Jason, who lives and teaches high school math in nearby Port Lavaca.

To Marilyn, Shara, Nancy, Shirley and Erica.
I love you all!

Chapter One

Was the driver crazy? At this rate he was going to hit her!

The headlights in Lucita Sanchez's rearview mirror were growing closer and closer, blinding her view of the secluded black highway in front of her.

Fear rifled through her, shooting adrenaline to every nerve in her body. Her knuckles in a white grip on the steering wheel, she pressed on the car's accelerator, hoping to pull away from the approaching vehicle.

Was the driver deliberately trying to ram into her? Maybe the driver couldn't see her?

Don't try to kid yourself, Lucita. Someone has been tailing you for weeks now. Long before you moved back to the Sandbur.

The broken white lines in the middle of the highway became one long blur as the speedometer crept toward ninety, then ninety-five. Behind her, the vehicle didn't appear to be relenting. Instead, the headlights seemed to be inching closer and closer to her back bumper.

Her mind was snatching for ways to escape when a jolt from behind lurched her forward in the seat and threatened to wrench the steering wheel from her grip.

The driver was ramming into her car! Someone was trying to kill her!

Dear God, what could she do? Obviously she couldn't outrun the other car. Even at this speed she was in dire danger of crashing. If she tried to pull over and stop, what would the driver do then? Stop and confront her?

She was frantically weighing the consequences of both choices when a black blob suddenly appeared directly in front of her on the highway.

Screaming, Lucita stomped on the brakes to avoid the animal. Her car instantly skidded sideways. Lights flashed as the vehicle spun round and round, end to end. The whipping momentum shot the car across the grassy right-of-way where it smashed through a fence, then crashed straight into an electric pole.

The violent jolt released the air bag and the safety device exploded in her face, the force snapping Lucita's head sideways against the window. She felt a stinging blow, and then she felt nothing at all.

Sometime later, she wasn't sure how long, awareness slowly returned to Lucita. Dazed, she struggled to push herself upright. The air bag had deflated and the nylon fabric was now draped uselessly against the steering wheel. Some sort of white powder was all over her. Apparently the stuff had exploded with the eruption of the air bag.

In front of her, steam was pouring from the crumpled

hood and raining down on the cracked windshield. Incredibly, the headlights were still burning, shining a wide swath of light into someone's pasture and illuminating several bulls grazing among a stand of tall mesquite trees.

Where was she? And what had happened?

Shoving strands of light brown hair off her face, she peered out the back windshield. More than fifty yards away, the highway was black and eerily quiet. Apparently no vehicles had passed since she'd rammed into the electric pole, or if anyone had driven by, they'd not stopped to help.

And what about the menacing vehicle that had been behind her? Whoever had been driving had obviously not stopped to offer her a helping hand when they'd witnessed her crash, which only proved the person had been out to do her harm.

With hands shaking violently, she felt along the left side of the dash and managed to turn off the headlights. The idiot who'd rammed into her just might decide to return and she didn't want the headlights of her disabled car to be shouting, here I am.

As total darkness settled around her, she realized the shoulder strap on the safety belt was biting into her throat. She reached for the buckle at her waist, then cursed beneath her breath as her fingers fumbled with the latch several times before she finally managed to unfasten it. Once she was free from the belt's restraint, she breathed a tiny sigh of relief.

Now, she needed to find her purse, she thought, as she tried to come up with a plan. Her cell phone was inside the bag. If all the jolting hadn't damaged it, she could get help within a few minutes.

Like a blind person, she flattened her hands and began to pat carefully along the seats and the floorboard. After several attempts, she finally discovered the handbag behind the passenger seat. Thankfully, the bag was zipped shut and the cell phone was exactly where she'd placed it.

When the instrument lit up, she sent up a silent prayer of thanks and quickly punched in 911. After informing the dispatcher of her accident and approximate location, she put the phone away and leaned back in the seat. Her family had gone to dinner at a neighbor's and she didn't want to bother them until she had to.

Lucita's mind tumbled with questions as to what to do next. Should she get out of the car to wait? Even though she didn't smell any fumes, the thing could be leaking gasoline, and any kind of spark might ignite flames. But knee-deep grass and weeds surrounded the car and rattlesnakes were as thick as rats in this area of Texas. Anyone with a lick of common sense wouldn't walk across their yard at night without a flashlight, much less wade through a tangle of vegetation on the side of the highway. If she had a flashlight to illuminate her steps, she might venture the trek from her car to the highway. But, damn it, she could never remember to keep one in the glove compartment.

Ten minutes later, she was growing restless and about to climb out of the car anyway, when a pickup truck with flashing lights atop the cab pulled off the shoulder of the highway. Relieved beyond measure, she reached for the door handle and realized with faint shock that the door was jammed. Quickly, she leaned across the seat and tried the passenger door—the only other door. It wouldn't budge. She couldn't have gotten out of the damn car even if she'd wanted to!

The bright orb of a flashlight suddenly passed over her window. Desperate now, Lucita turned on the key and pressed the electronic button to lower the thick glass.

"I can't open the door!" she called out to the tall figure approaching the car.

"Just stay where you are. I'll be there in a second."

The male voice was strong and solid and very reassuring. Relief tumbled through her, and for one brief moment she feared she was going to weep.

Don't fall apart now, Lucita. You've dealt with far worse crises than this.

The officer finally managed to wade through the tangle of grass and weeds until he reached the side of her wrecked car. Pointing his flashlight straight at her face, he asked, "Are you injured? The dispatcher said an ambulance wasn't needed."

Closing her eyes against the blinding light, she said, "I think I'm okay. Just shaken. Both doors seemed to be stuck. Can you get me out of here?"

He tried the driver's door and after a few strong jerks, the latch broke free. Quickly grabbing her handbag, Lucita swung her legs to the ground. With the help of his hand on her arm, she pushed herself out of the car.

"Ooooh." Too woozy to stand, she instinctively reached for the nearest solid thing to steady herself, which just happened to be the officer's broad chest.

"Whoa!" he urged. "Don't faint on me now!"

His reflexes were quick, and suddenly she felt a pair of massive arms wrapping around her, hugging her against the solid length of his body.

"Easy, ma'am. Take a few deep breaths. Slow and steady."

She did as he commanded. After a few moments she could feel her strength returning, and with it the embarrassment that she'd practically collapsed into a strange man's arms.

Beneath her cheek, the starched fabric of his shirt was cool and smooth and smelled of musk and sweetgrasses. In contrast, his arms were warm and their strong support made her feel safer than she'd felt in a long, long time.

Chiding herself for the moment of weakness, she forced her cheek away from his chest. "I—I'm fine. I'm sure I can stand on my own now," she insisted.

He dropped his arms, but kept a careful hand on her elbow. "I'm Deputy Ripp McCleod, ma'am, with the Goliad County Sheriff's Department. And you are?"

McCleod? Years ago there had been a sheriff with that name. Could they be related? "Lucita Sanchez. I live on the Sandbur."

His fingers were so long they wrapped completely around her arm. In spite of her claim that she was fine, she was inwardly grateful for the deputy's steadying hand. Otherwise, she wasn't sure her shaky legs had regained enough strength to keep her totally upright.

"You're related to Matt and Cordero?"

It wasn't a big surprise to hear this man call her brothers by their given names. Most South Texans were familiar with the Sandbur ranch. This lawman was probably a native of Goliad County. More than likely, he knew many people who lived and worked on the ranch. He just wouldn't remember her. Not since she'd been gone from her family home for several years and had only just returned in the past few months.

Quickly, she pulled her license and insurance verification from her purse to hand it to the deputy.

"Yes," she answered. "Matt and Cordero are my brothers. I—I was on my way home when this happened." She waved her arm toward the front of the car. She hadn't uprooted the electric pole with her car's assault, but it was listing toward the west at a precarious angle. The heavy wires were sagging, though thankfully none of them were touching the ground. Cedar posts from the fence she'd run through were now lying on their sides, along with several strands of barbed wire. It was a miracle none of the bulls had milled onto the highway.

The deputy's thoughts were clearly running along the same path as hers as he twisted his head toward a two-way radio fastened to his shoulder. "Hey, Lijah, hurry up. We got cattle here with a fence down. Get it up as quick as you can before they cause more accidents. And you need to call the power company and let them know a pole needs to be reset."

"Roger, will do," the officer answered. "I can see your lights now. Anyone hurt?"

"Don't think so."

Deputy McCleod turned his attention back to Lucita and the vague notion that she'd seen him somewhere before raced through her mind. "Is there anyone else in the car?"

It was a hot, moonless night with thin clouds blocking out the stars. The only glimpses Lucita could get of the deputy's face were when his flashlight inadvertently bobbed upward. Yet in spite of the lack of lighting, she could see that he was a tall man, even after factoring in his dark cowboy hat. His broad shoulders were covered with a uniform-type shirt made of khaki. Blue jeans encased his long, strong legs, while black, square-toed cowboy boots peeped from beneath the hems. A leather gun belt strapped some sort of revolver low on his slim hips. He was the epitome of a Texas lawman, making her acutely aware of his authoritative presence.

"No," she said. "I was traveling alone."

"Can you tell me what happened? Or do you remember?" he asked.

He had one of those soft, gravelly voices that made her want to shiver. Or was that reaction from the shock she'd been through? Either way, she hugged her arms against her breasts.

"I'm not totally sure—something ran in front of me. A wild hog, I think. Did you see one on the highway?" She twisted her head in the direction of the darkened blacktop. "I hope I didn't hit it."

"I didn't see a hog on the road or the shoulders. Only a set of skid marks a country mile long. You must have been mighty anxious to get home. Just how fast were you going, Ms. Sanchez?"

There was a hint of censure in his voice, which could only be expected. No one in his right mind would drive the speed she'd been traveling on the highway at night. *Except someone in fear for her life,* she thought grimly.

"Too fast," she conceded. "But I—it's not like you think. I wasn't just in a hurry to get to the ranch. I was—"

Before she could go on, he interrupted, "In this area, wildlife on the highway is a major problem—even while driving the speed limit."

He didn't have to tell Lucita that. This patch of Texas had been her home for many years before she'd moved to Corpus. She'd seen plenty of mangled vehicles and even deaths caused by wandering wildlife.

"Yes, I'm aware of that, Deputy. But I—" How could she tell him that she believed someone had been deliberately trying to run her off the road? Even to herself, the notion sounded incredible. And because she had no evidence to back up her suspicion, she kept it to herself.

Wearily, she reached up to push her long hair away from her face. As her fingertips brushed past her temple, they encountered something wet and sticky. She felt around on her head for the source of the gooey substance and yelped when her fingers pushed onto a lump and an open gash.

"Oww!" Lifting her hand in front of her face, she could see blood smeared on her fingers. "I must have cut myself."

"Let me take a look."

Stepping forward, he directed the light toward the side of her head. Lucita stood rigidly still while he parted her long hair to examine the wound. Once again she was assaulted with the pleasant smell of his shirt, the masculine strength of his warm body.

"Yeah, that's a pretty nasty gash. It was hidden by your hair and I didn't see it before," he murmured. "I'd better call in an ambulance, after all. You might need to be checked for a concussion."

She deliberately moved back from him. "Forget it. I'm not comfortable with hospitals. Besides, my cousin and her husband are both doctors. They'll come to the ranch and check me out if need be."

"I'm concerned about more than a concussion," he said in a brusque, businesslike voice. "You're probably going to need stitches, too."

Before she could guess his intention, he pulled a

handkerchief from his pocket, gathered one corner together and pressed the fabric to the wound.

His big hand inadvertently brushed against her cheek and she closed her eyes as she tried to steel herself against the odd emotions rushing through her. How long had it been since a man who wasn't related to her had been this close? Three years. Three long, lonely years.

"I'll make sure I get the wound cared for, Deputy. Thank you."

Sensing that he was making her uncomfortable, he handed the handkerchief to her and stepped back.

"Be sure that you do." Curling his fingers around her upper arm, he asked, "Can you make it over to my truck? I need to write up the accident and you'll be more comfortable there."

Sitting down would be a relief. At the moment it was an effort for her to remain upright. Her head must have taken a harder whack than she'd thought. The dizziness and nausea she'd felt the moment she'd stood on her feet was still coming and going in great waves. "I think so," she told him.

With his hand on her arm, he supported most of her weight as the two of them waded through the tall grass and weeds. Just as they reached his truck, another patrol car braked to a jarring halt at the side of the highway.

An officer climbed out of the vehicle and Deputy McCleod called over to him.

"If you haven't already called for a tow truck, do that now, then deal with the fence."

The other man lifted a hand in acknowledgment.

The deputy led Lucita around to the passenger door of his truck, which he'd left idling, and helped her into the seat. Once she was inside and he'd shut the door behind her, she began to shiver, but whether her reaction was from the air-conditioning blowing from the dash or anticipation of a grilling, she wasn't sure. She just knew she wanted this whole ordeal over with so that she could go home to her family.

Lights of all shapes and colors illuminated knobs and meters on the dashboard in front of her. A two-way radio crackled as voices intermittently sent information across the airwaves. Behind her head, against the back windshield, long, high-powered rifles rested in a gun rack. She wondered if the lawman had ever been forced to use any of his weapons.

Seconds later, the deputy was sliding into the seat next to her. He switched on the interior cab light and the small space was filled with a dim, yellowish glow. She studied his profile as he silently reached for a clipboard and began to copy information from her driver's license.

The man was somewhere in his mid to late thirties, Lucita decided. A strong, square jaw was covered with a faint stubble of dark whiskers. Coffee-brown sideburns ended at the lobes of his ears while his hair was just long enough to curl against his nape. His nose was on the large side and surprisingly straight for a man who'd undoubtedly been involved in a fair share of physical scuffles. Faint creases bracketed a roughly hewn set of lips, which at the moment were pressed together in a grim line. No doubt he was very unhappy with her careless driving.

Head still bent, he continued to write. "I don't think I need to point out how lucky you were tonight. I think you already realize you could have been killed."

Lucita drew in a deep breath. She wished she could see his eyes. They might give her a clue as to what he was actually thinking. But they were totally shadowed by the brim of his hat. Her gaze fell to his left hand. The ring finger was blank. But what did that matter? Why was she even wondering if the man was married?

She tried to focus on the real reason for sitting next to this lanky deputy. He seemed like a strong, capable man and something about his presence gave her a sense of security. She needed to tell him what actually happened on the highway. She needed his help. Otherwise, she might not survive. "Looking at it that way, I suppose you're right. But at the moment I don't especially feel lucky. I—you see, only moments before my encounter with the hog, there was a car tailgating me. It got so close that it bumped me."

Turning his head, he looked directly at her. The full view of his face was almost as jolting as hitting the power pole, she decided.

"Bumped you?"

Even though he'd only spoken two words, she could hear disbelief in his voice. Looking at it from his view, she could see how ridiculous it sounded. This was a rural area where most people lived at a slow pace. Neighbor knew neighbor and they definitely didn't try to run one another off the road.

"Yes. At first the lights were so bright and close I was practically blinded. I sped up to try to get ahead of them, but the car wouldn't back off. Finally it got so close, it rammed my bumper—hard enough to nearly wrench the steering wheel from my hands. I was trying to decide whether to try to outrun it or simply pull over and stop when the hog ran in front of me. I swerved to miss it, and my car began to spin. The next thing I knew, the front end was wrapped around the power pole."

His gaze dropped back to the clipboard. "Are you sure the vehicle actually bumped you? This particular highway has a few potholes. Hitting one at a high rate of speed can cause serious jolts and even accidents."

Feeling more blood trickling through her hair, she pressed his handkerchief more firmly to the wound on her head. "I understand that this all sounds unbelievable. But it wasn't a pothole. The car really did bash into me."

As though he needed a closer inspection of her, he turned toward her as his thumb pushed the brim of his hat a fraction higher on his forehead. "Did you have any sort of altercation with this vehicle before the accident? Maybe you forgot to dim your lights and the driver got angry and wanted payback? Or you cut them off from a prime parking space? Unfortunately, road rage can get out of hand."

Shaking her head, she said firmly, "No. Nothing like that happened today, yesterday or any time."

A faint dimple grooved his cheek as he smiled. "You must be a very courteous driver, Ms. Sanchez."

Looking away from him, she reminded herself that she'd never been attracted to lawmen, that they were too cocky for her taste. This one was no exception. Still, there was something about him that affected her in the most sensual sort of way.

"Most Texans are courteous drivers," she replied. "Except for the idiot chasing me."

He glanced thoughtfully out the windshield. "If this wasn't a case of road rage, then why would someone be chasing you? Have you had a personal dispute with anyone?"

His questions made her squirm uncomfortably. She realized the more she tried to explain the accident tonight, the stranger she sounded. "I realize I must seem paranoid to you, or worse, a woman suffering from histrionics. But I've been—I believe that someone has been following me around. Stalking me."

She glanced over to see he was staring at her with genuine concern. She was relieved he was actually taking her fears seriously.

"Have you reported this to the authorities?" he asked.

"No." She probably should have, but without proof, law officials would have considered her a paranoid loon or something. Besides, she'd continued to hope the whole matter would simply go away.

"What about your family? Did you tell any of them about this?"

"I mentioned it to my aunt Geraldine. But at that time, it was only a feeling on my part."

His dark gaze continued to search her face as though he was trying to see the truth. She could have told him he wouldn't find anything underneath her skin. She was just a plain, totally forgettable schoolteacher.

"Do you have any enemies that you're aware of?"

Lucita released a long, pent-up breath. "Not really. But in this day and age, how does anyone ever know? I do teach high school in Victoria at St. Francis. I suppose an angry student could be wanting to scare me."

"Scaring is one thing, but stalking is a criminal act and very serious."

The long chase she'd gone through tonight had certainly felt criminal. But she didn't want to think about that now. She didn't want to think that someone might have actually wanted to scare her that much, or even worse, to make her crash.

She tried to shake off the sinister thoughts. "Well, the car did go on after I crashed. I suppose if the driver had really wanted to do me harm they would have come back to finish what they started."

The deputy's lips pressed into a grim line. "I don't want to scare you, but this person might have believed the crash finished you and he or she didn't want to risk being caught at the scene of a crime."

Lucita's blood turned ice-cold. "I can only hope you're wrong."

His expression softened slightly. "I hope I'm wrong, too," he replied, then asked, "Can you tell me more about the vehicle?"

Shaking her head, she sighed wearily. "Not much. I'm fairly certain that it was a car, low-slung and sleek. It looked black or some dark color."

"Nothing more about the make or model? The tag?"

A dull ache was beginning to spread through her whole head. She wiped a hand over her forehead while wishing for aspirin and a cool pillow beneath her cheek. "No. I didn't have time to catch any details. It zoomed up behind me and then I was too blinded to see anything more."

Nodding, he jotted something down on his notepad. "Well, right now you're probably going to be more angry with me than the tailgater, because I'm going to have to write you up on a traffic violation for reckless driving."

Wide-eyed now, she stared at him. "What about the hog? Doesn't it count for anything? And the tailgater—or whatever he was?"

One corner of his mouth lifted wryly. "Other than

your word, I have no proof of a tailgater or a hog. But I do intend to make a search." He handed her info back to her, then, picking up the flashlight, he opened the truck door and ordered, "You stay where you are."

What the heck did he think she was going to do? Lucita wondered. Her car was incapacitated and her legs felt like mush. It was still several miles to the ranch. She could hardly walk home from here. And she wasn't about to stumble around in the dark to help him hunt for a dead hog.

Far off to her left, beneath a beam of headlights, she could see her crumpled car and the officer called Lijah working to upright the barbed-wire fence. To her immediate right, Deputy McCleod was searching the shoulders of the highway, sweeping the high grass with his flashlight.

The man was a handsome devil, she thought. There was no denying the fact. Something about this man had caught her attention the moment he'd stepped up and dabbed his handkerchief to her bleeding head.

She still couldn't believe she'd actually searched his left hand for a sign of a wedding ring. What could have possibly possessed her? The deputy's marital status had nothing to do with anything.

She wasn't looking for a man to curl up to. Even one that looked as good as Deputy Ripp McCleod. She'd had one good-looking, smooth-talking man in her life and now that he'd gone with the wind, along with her family inheritance, she'd vowed to never have another. But this Texas lawman was more than enough to make a woman forget her vows!

Chapter Two

Her head now throbbing with pain, Lucita pulled her handbag onto her lap and began to search for a pain-killer. She was still pawing her way through lipstick tubes and crumpled receipts when the cab door opened again and Deputy McCleod slid beneath the steering wheel. With him came the warm night air and his distinctly male scent. A prickle of awareness suddenly dotted her skin with goose bumps.

"No hog, Ms. Sanchez," he told her. "Once it's daylight, the department will have a closer inspection of your car. Of course, if we find anything, we'll inform you."

She let out a breath she hadn't realized she was holding. "Actually, I'm glad you didn't find the hog. I didn't want to think I'd ended its life, even if it would have helped me avoid a ticket."

He reached for the clipboard and the paper where

he'd jotted down her license information. "Hog. Tail-gater. Whatever. You were obviously driving way too fast, Ms. Sanchez. I'd say if you put any value on that neck of yours, you'd better slow down."

Lucita clamped her lips together as she watched him scratch more comments across the bottom of a second set of documents. He was right, but that didn't make it any easier to watch him write what looked to be a whole stack of driving tickets.

"What am I supposed to do if someone starts to harass me on the highway again?" she asked with a hint of sarcasm.

He looked up and Lucita couldn't help but notice the way his dark brows met in the middle of his forehead, the way the corners of his chiseled lips turned faintly downward. The man even made frowning look sexy, she thought.

"You really are concerned about a stalker, aren't you?"

She nodded. "It's just a hunch, but enough of one to scare me."

To her surprise he reached across the seat and gently touched her forearm in a reassuring way. "I wouldn't borrow trouble, Ms. Sanchez. Unfortunately, lots of people encounter rude, reckless drivers on the highway, but that's where it ends. I doubt you'll have any more problems. Just be vigilant and drive safely."

Under normal circumstances, Lucita would agree with him. But her past wasn't exactly normal. Three years ago her ex-husband had stolen every penny of the inheritance her family had given her after she'd turned twenty-five. And so far the police hadn't been able to locate his whereabouts. But she wasn't about to get into that sordid story with this man. After all, Deputy McCleod considered this a traffic incident and nothing more. And perhaps it would be best to let him keep thinking that, Lucita decided. Especially when she hadn't a lick of proof that the person who'd practically run her down on the highway was Derek Campbell or anyone connected to him. Besides, during their ten-year marriage he'd never once threatened to harm her in any way.

Yet for the past few weeks she hadn't been able to shake the idea that her ex was somehow connected to the person who'd been shadowing her comings and goings.

Folding the lawman's handkerchief into a tight square, Lucita pressed it back to the leaky wound on the side of her head. "You're right, Deputy McCleod," she said after a moment. "I need to quit worrying and be glad that my car was the only victim tonight."

"Like I said earlier, you're one fortunate lady," he said in a low voice. "I guess you know that?"

"Yeah," she said with feigned cheerfulness, "this is definitely my lucky night." Straightening her back, she looked away from him and said, "If you're finished writing up that report, I'm going to call my brother to come get me."

"That won't be necessary," he said curtly. "I'm taking you home myself."

Her head turned toward him. "What?"

"We're not that far from the Sandbur," he explained. "There's no need to bother your family. Besides, I think I need to talk with them about this little accident."

Lucita couldn't help but stare at him and wonder at his motive. As far as she knew, it wasn't the legal responsibility of the sheriff's department to see that she got home safely. "Is that normal procedure?" she couldn't help but ask.

His face stoic, he ripped her portion of the ticket from his clipboard and handed it over to her. She took the piece of paper and without a glance crammed it into her purse.

"There's no need for you to concern yourself about my procedure, Ms. Sanchez. I never step out of bounds."

With the law, or women? she wondered. But she kept that question to herself. If this man knew she'd been looking at him as anything other than an official of the law, he'd probably write her a second set of tickets.

Deputy McCleod twisted the key in the ignition and the truck sparked to life. As he whirled the vehicle onto the highway, he picked up the two-way mike fastened to the dashboard. "Lijah, I'm headed to the Sandbur. Be sure to measure the skid marks and try to locate the owner of the damaged fence. If those bulls get out we'll have accidents and lawsuits all over the place."

"Gotcha, Ripp. Will do."

Grabbing the seat belt, Lucita fastened it across her lap while the deputy gunned the truck down the highway toward the Sandbur turnoff.

Once she had the belt securely in place, she settled against the seat and stared out the blackened windshield. Her throbbing pulse was causing the gash on her head to leak even more and she pressed the handkerchief tightly to the wound. The fleeting thought passed through her mind that the snow-white fabric he'd lent her would never be the same again. She would owe him a handkerchief. But would she ever have the opportunity to repay him?

Idiot, she scolded herself. Seeing Deputy McCleod again was the last thing she needed to be thinking about.

From the corner of her eye, she watched him reach for the two-way radio. After the female dispatcher responded he began repeating letters and numbers that Lucita quickly recognized from her car tag and driver's license. She understood. Even though her family was well-known in this part of Texas, he had no way of knowing if she had outstanding tickets or warrants. He had to treat her like any other person involved in an accident.

Moments later the dispatcher came back on the air. "Everything clear on that license and tag, number two."

"Roger. Thanks."

"Did she call you number two?" Lucita asked curiously.

"That's my code," he explained. "I'm the chief deputy behind the sheriff."

"Oh." She should have guessed he wasn't a mere deputy. The man reeked authority, along with all that masculinity.

"Where will my car be taken?" she asked after a moment.

He answered her question. "To the only salvage yard in town—Santee's. But just in case you're wondering, I can save you the trouble and tell you right now that the vehicle is totaled."

He flipped on the left-hand blinker and turned onto a graveled road that would eventually carry them to Lucita's family ranch. The Sandbur was such a large property that it was divided into two: the Mission River Division and the Goliad Division. The latter was where the homes of the owners were located and it was to that bustling part of the ranch that Deputy McCleod headed as he guided the truck over a bumpy road past stands of mesquite trees and wesatch bushes.

Lucita wanted to ask him who'd made him an authority on automobiles, but she bit her tongue. There wasn't any point in taking her bad fortune out on this lawman. So far he'd treated her with respect and concern where another lawman might have taken pleasure in giving her an angry chewing-out.

Forcing her gaze away from his handsome profile, she said in a quiet voice, "Do you think I'm lying about the tailgater bumping into me?"

Not bothering to spare her a glance, he said, "No. But there's a chance you could be mistaken. Things happen quickly when a person is traveling at a high rate of speed. And I—"

He paused as though he didn't think his next words were appropriate and Lucita was quick to prompt him. "Please finish, Deputy McCleod. I respect your experienced opinion."

"Okay. I get the feeling that you're holding something back about this whole thing."

The insinuation in his words made her more than a little uncomfortable. She didn't want this man knowing that she was the black sheep of the Saddler-Sanchez family, that she was the only one who'd brought shame upon herself and her loved ones by marrying a guy they all objected to. "In other words, you don't trust me."

He darted a glance at her and the aloofness on his face left her colder than the air blowing from the vents on the dashboard.

"Ms. Sanchez, in my business I can't take anyone at face value."

Thankfully for Lucita the remaining distance to the ranch house was only a few short miles. The atmosphere inside the deputy's truck was thick with tension and the only noise breaking the awkward silence was the sound of crackling voices going back and forth over the two-way radio.

Lucita hunkered down and tried to rest her head on the back of the seat, but each time the truck hit a washed-out hole in the road, the jarring seemed to go right to her injury. After a couple of minutes she gave up and sat rigidly on the edge of the seat.

Before long they crossed a cattle guard framed with an iron pipe entrance. Above, on the arch brace, the S/S brand cut from sheet metal swung in the night breeze.

After they rumbled across the slatted cattle guard, the road began to branch off in all directions between barns, corrals and outbuildings. Deputy McCleod seemed to know exactly where he was going, as he passed the main ranch house, and barreled on toward her father's redbrick home. She could only surmise that he'd been here before. Perhaps he'd visited when some unidentified ruffians had seriously injured her father in town, or maybe he was acquainted with her brothers personally. She could only guess. One thing she did know, if she'd met him before, she would have never forgotten him.

Lucita quickly corrected his directions. "I'm not living with my father and brothers. I live in the guest-house out back. You need to go past the first turnoff."

Thankfully he didn't ply her with personal questions. Instead, he said, "I think I'd better hand you over to your family, first. I want to make sure you get that wound attended to."

The man didn't even trust her to take care of herself. Well, what did she expect, she asked herself grimly. She'd confessed to driving at dangerous speeds. That didn't exactly speak well for her common sense. But if he'd only seen the menacing car trying to run her down, he might actually understand the desperation she'd felt.

Moments later he parked in front of the Grecian-style manor house. Grabbing up her handbag, Lucita followed him up the lighted path to the front entrance. She hoped that someone was home by now.

To her relief, her older brother, Matteo, Matt to those who knew him well, answered the door. The moment he saw the caller was Deputy McCleod, he stepped onto the concrete porch with a broad smile and reached to shake his hand.

"Ripp! What are you doing out here tonight, old buddy?"

The tall, lean deputy stepped to one side and gestured to Lucita, who was standing at the edge of the shadows.

"I have your sister here, Matt. She met up with an accident a little bit earlier tonight. I thought you'd better know about it."

Lucita felt like a child bringing home a note from her teacher. Only this was worse than getting caught rubbing dirt in a boy's face or kicking a pompous cheerleader in the shins.

For a moment her dark-haired, muscular brother was completely stunned. "My God! Luci!"

Stepping into the glaring orb of the porch light, Lucita realized she must be a frightful sight. Blood was smeared on her cheek and hands, and at some point since the accident, it had dripped onto her beige blouse and matching slacks, leaving red splotches against the expensive linen.

Matt grabbed her by the shoulders. "What happened?"

Even though Matt was only four years older than her

thirty-six years, he took the big brother role a step further, treating her more like a father. For the past three years it had been Matt who'd pestered and cajoled until she'd packed up her son and their belongings and moved from Corpus Christi back to the Sandbur. It had been Matt who'd convinced her that family was meant to be together, especially in times of trouble. Well, she'd had more than her share of strife and it looked as though her misfortune was still hanging around to make her life even more difficult.

"I'm okay, Matt. Really. It's just a little cut on the head. Is Marti inside or at the guesthouse?" She glanced around him to the double door entrance of the house. If her eleven-year-old son, Marti, spotted the official sheriff vehicle in the driveway, he'd be outside in a split second to investigate. Lucita wasn't keen about him seeing her in such a state. The boy had already been through enough traumas these past three years without him knowing his mother had nearly lost her life.

"Neither. He and Gracia are up at the big house playing some sort of card game with Aunt Geraldine."

"Good," she said, relieved. "I don't want him to see me like this."

Matt whipped an accusing look at the deputy. "Ripp, what the hell did you bring her here for? She needs to be in the emergency room!"

Ripp grimaced. He'd expected this from Matt. And no doubt Mingo would be just as appalled to see his daughter battered and bleeding. The Sanchez men were one of the reasons he'd decided to personally deliver Lucita here to the ranch. Several years ago, Mingo had gone out of his way to help Ripp get the job of Chief Deputy for Sheriff Travers. As for Matt, he'd become a friend to Ripp while in high school and that friendship had deepened over the years. During that time he'd not met Lucita, but now he definitely wished he had.

"Your sister is just as bullheaded as you are, Matt. She refused an ambulance. Said her cousin would sew her up if need be."

"Luci, there are times to be tough, and then there're times you need to accept help! When are you ever going to learn that?" Matt gently scolded before grabbing his sister by the arm and hurrying her toward the house. "You lucked out tonight, sis. Nicci and Ridge just happened to come back with us after supper and they're still here." He looked over to Ripp. "Come in, Ripp. You can tell me what happened while Nicci sees to Luci's injury."

Nodding, Ripp followed the two siblings inside the big, two-story house. Compared to Ripp's little bungalow on the outskirts of Goliad, this home was more than a mansion. The Saddler and Sanchez families, co-owners of the Sandbur, were wealthy and had been for more than a century. Yet Ripp would be the first to admit that Matt and his family never behaved as though they were affluent. Whenever he'd been around them, they had acted the same as any regular folks that worked hard for a living. And Ripp knew for a fact that none of the men sat back and let the hired help run the ranch for them. They got manure on their hands just like the rest of the crew. But as for their sister, Lucita, Ripp was in the dark. Before tonight he'd heard snippets of gossip about her from time to time. Lucita seemed to be the outsider of the family, but then a person could hear anything, especially when they worked in law enforcement.

"Nicci! Juliet! Come here!" Matt yelled as they stepped into an empty great room.

Matt's wife Juliet, a tall blond woman, was the first to rush into the room. Nicci, their pregnant cousin, was right behind her and with her doctor's instinct, she was the first to race to Lucita.

"My God, Lucita!" Nicci exclaimed. "What happened?"

"Seems she's had some sort of car accident," Matt spoke up before Lucita could answer. "Can you do something about her head?"

"Of course! Ridge and I carry a medical bag around in the car—just in case it's needed. I'll get him to fetch it." The petite brunette gently placed her arm around Lucita's shoulder. "Come on, Luci, let's get that wound taken care of."

Juliet started toward the kitchen. "I'll tell Ridge to get the medical bag."

Once the three women were out of the room, Ripp watched Matt heave out a heavy sigh before turning a look of concern on him.

"What in hell happened, Ripp? Were any other cars involved?"

"I'm not exactly sure about that."

Matt raked a hand through his hair and Ripp thought his friend seemed a little overwrought about the whole incident. True, his sister had been slightly injured and her car was smashed, but that was a minor problem to a family with money to spare.

"What the hell does that mean?"

"We'll talk about that later. Right now you should just be happy that all Lucita received was a bump on the head. She's lucky to be alive. Before we left the scene of the accident, she admitted to me that she'd been driving very fast."

His face grim, Matt stared at him. "So she was breaking the speed limit, after sundown, when she knows the deer and hogs are venturing out? What the hell was she thinking?"

Ripp grimaced. He hated being the bearer of bad news, but in this case and every case, he had to be honest even if it meant bringing worry and pain to a friend.

"I'm not sure. Hell, Matt, she left skid marks from here to the horse barn and that's no exaggeration. I haven't examined the scene of the accident closely yet, I left Lijah in charge of that. But on first glance it looked as though once she stomped on the brakes, the car went into a spin. The front wound up having a head-on crash with a power pole. Her vehicle is totaled, that's for sure."

Shaking his head with disbelief, Matt gestured toward a grouping of leather furniture situated in front of a fireplace—unlit, of course, since they were presently sweating through the last sultry days of August.

"Sit, Ripp. We don't need to stand up to talk. How about a cup of coffee or a beer?"

Ripp really didn't have time to sit or enjoy any sort of drink, but Matt seemed particularly upset about his sister's accident. He didn't want to make things worse for him by cutting this visit short. "Better make it coffee," he told his friend. "I'm still on duty."

While Ripp made himself comfortable in a nearby armchair, Matt left for the kitchen. As he waited for the rancher to return, Ripp slowly eyed the spacious room. He'd been in the house a few times in the past few years and what he always remembered most about the place was that, in spite of the opulence, its rooms were warm, relaxed and homey.

Lucita had told him that she lived in the guesthouse situated about a hundred yards behind this building. He'd never been inside that particular house, but it had always reminded him of one of those Mediterranean villas with its low roof, pale pink stucco and arched supports running along the ground-floor porch. To Ripp it was a minimansion, but it didn't compare to this house and he wondered why the sister and her son had chosen to live there instead of here with the rest of the family. Maybe those rumors he'd heard about her being an outsider of sorts were true. Or maybe her husband didn't want to live that closely with his in-laws. That is, if she had a husband. The name on her driver's license had been Sanchez and nothing more. But there were some women who chose not to take their husbands' name, especially when they were from a prestigious family, whose name equaled authority.

In any case, he shouldn't be curious about the woman. She was a ranching heiress, a woman way out of a poor lawman's league, and more than likely married. So why had something about her caught his attention from the very first moment he'd walked up to her demolished car?

Maybe because she's a beauty and then some, McCleod. And maybe because when she fell into your arms you felt an overwhelming sense of protectiveness.

Moments later, when Matt reappeared in the living room, Ripp did his best to shake away his strange feelings toward his friend's sister.

A young woman with a black braid wound atop her head followed him, carrying a tray with an insulated pot and two cups.

"Sorry for keeping you waiting, Ripp," Matt said as

he took a seat on the couch. "Alida was making fresh coffee and I was explaining to Dad about the accident."

Ripp looked toward the kitchen. "Where is your father?"

Matt jerked his head toward the part of the house where the women had disappeared. "He and Ridge are checking on Luci."

Alida, the young maid, quietly served each man a mug full of coffee then discreetly left the room. Once she was out of sight, Matt scooted to the edge of the seat and pinned Ripp with an insistent stare.

"All right, Ripp, what's the real story here? I can see it on your face. Something else was going on with Luci tonight, wasn't it?"

Ripp's dark brows slowly inched upward. "What do you mean? Your sister had a wreck. It happens to a lot of people—unfortunately every day of the year."

"Damn it, man, that's not what I mean! What did she tell you caused it? My sister isn't irresponsible. On top of that, she's a careful driver. She wouldn't have been speeding just because she wanted to go fast. Luci would be too worried about hurting someone else on the highway to do such a thing. She's that sort of person."

Ripp took a sip of the rich, Colombian coffee as he met Matt's gaze with a frank look. "Your sister said someone was tailgating her—trying to hit her from behind. She said she sped up in an attempt to get away from the other vehicle. After that, a hog ran in front of her and she tried to avoid hitting it. That's when she lost control of the car."

As Ripp talked he could see his friend's expression grow harder and harder. Strange, he thought, that Matt hadn't responded with disbelief.

"What about the other car?" Matt asked.

Ripp shrugged. "If there was another car it apparently went on down the highway."

"And didn't bother to see if anyone had been hurt? Doesn't that seem a bit strange?"

Actually, Lucita's Sanchez's whole rendition of the accident had seemed outlandish to Ripp, but in his line of work he'd seen stranger things happen out on the roads and highways. "Only a little, Matt. Lots of people don't want to get involved with accidents."

"Fender benders maybe. But from what you tell me this was a crash! Someone could have been dead!"

Ripp took another sip of coffee as he measured his friend's strong reaction. He tried to make his next question as casual sounding as he could. "Do you believe someone was actually trying to run your sister off the road?"

"Damn right, I believe it," Matt snapped. "If she said it, then it happened. Luci doesn't lie."

Trying to keep an open mind about the whole thing, Ripp said, "All right, Matt, if you say so, I believe you. So I'm asking as a lawman, is there some reason you believe Lucita was attacked?"

Lucita's brother stared down into his mug. "Not exactly," he said quietly.

"That's funny," Ripp replied. "I got the impression that you weren't too surprised to hear about Lucita's claims. And she tells me she believes someone has been stalking her."

With a tight grimace, Matt lifted his gaze up to Ripp's. "Look, Ripp, my sister…" His words trailing away, he glanced over his shoulder to make sure no one else had entered the room. "She's had a rough time of things for a few years now. I don't want to say a lot about it, because frankly, she's not wild about everyone knowing what went on between her and that bastard of a husband she used to have."

Used to have. Crazy, how Ripp's mind had latched onto those three words. "Your sister is divorced?"

Matt nodded. "Yeah. And I thank God she is. He was a loser and—"

"And what?" Ripp prompted, realizing he wanted to know more about the lovely woman who'd fallen briefly into his arms. She'd felt soft and fragile and her hair had smelled like the flowers that had grown in his mother's garden. He knew his reaction to her was sappy, even foolish, but it was there and he couldn't stop it.

"Well, nobody knows where he is," Matt went on. "He disappeared."

Frowning, Ripp tried to understand what significance that had on Lucita's car accident. "Hell, Matt, that's not so unusual. Especially if he had to pay alimony."

Matt's expression was suddenly thunderous. "It's not alimony I'm talking about—they have a son. Marti thinks his father hates him. That's hell for an eleven-year-old boy."

Lucita had a son. He figured something like that while they'd been on the porch and she'd mentioned the name Marti. But she was divorced. That snippet of information put everything in a different light. A light that he needed to switch off, he quickly reminded himself.

"Has her ex ever stalked her before?"

Matt shook his head. "No. Not that I know of."

"What about threats or anything like that?" Ripp persisted. If there was even the slightest chance that Lucita Sanchez was in danger, he wanted to know about it.

More thoughtful now than angry, Matt said, "No, Lucita has never mentioned anything like that. In fact, I'm sure she hasn't heard from him since he left."

"Well, this whole thing could have just been an accident, Matt. There're some pretty foolish drivers out there on the road. They might not have realized just how close they were to your sister. In any case, I wouldn't worry myself about it."

He drained the last of his coffee and placed the mug on a nearby end table. "I'd better be going, Matt. I left Lijah dealing with the fence your sister plowed up. He might need help."

Ripp started toward the foyer and Matt followed. At the door, the rancher slapped a grateful hand on his shoulder.

"Thanks for bringing Lucita home, Ripp. We'll see that she's taken care of."

Nodding, Ripp said, "A tow truck will take her car into Santee's. After the sheriff's department finishes its investigation, Lucita's insurance company can find it there." He grimaced as he glanced back at his friend. "Sorry, Matt, but I had to give her a citation. Without proof of the other car I couldn't do anything else."

"I wouldn't expect you to do anything else," Matt said, and then with a worried shake of his head, added, "I just hope nothing else happens and that it really was only some nutty driver on the road."

"Yeah. Me, too," Ripp agreed.

Realizing he'd already stayed longer than he should have, Ripp gave Matt a final farewell and left the house. But as he drove away, his gaze drifted one last time to the scattered lights beaming through the windows of the

Sanchez home. A part of him wished he could have seen Lucita before he'd left. Just to make sure she was okay.

Forget her, McCleod. You don't want another woman in your life. Especially a gorgeous heiress with problems as big as her bank account. That sort of trouble you don't need.

Ripp was agreeing with the little voice in his head and trying to push her pretty face from his mind when Lijah's voice suddenly came across the radio.

"Hey, number two. You close to your radio?"

Sighing with unexplained weariness, Ripp picked up the mike. "Yeah. I'm here, Lijah. What's up? You didn't let those bulls get out, did you?"

"Forget the fence. Done got it patched. I've been measuring those skid marks like you told me, but I've run into a little problem."

Ripp frowned. Lijah wasn't always the smartest deputy on the crew, but Ripp loved him like a brother and tried to be patient with his sometimes-thick head. "What sort of problem?"

"There're two sets of skid marks here, Ripp."

Ripp's mind whirled as he tried to recall the marks he'd inspected from inside his truck as he'd driven up to the scene of the accident. He'd not taken the time to stop and walk the whole distance of the tire tracks. At that time it had been more important to make sure the occupants of the car were okay. Apparently Lijah had found something to corroborate Lucita's story. "Two? Take a closer look, Lijah. You got your glasses on?"

"Dang it, Ripp, you know I don't come to work without my glasses! I see two sets of skid marks. They're almost on top of each other. You'd better come look for yourself."

A cold, sinking feeling dropped to the pit of Ripp's stomach. This was evidence that another car had been following Lucita closely. But did it mean that someone had been trying to harm her? He couldn't answer that with one hundred percent certainty until he investigated more. And that was something he thoroughly intended to do.

"Lay out some barriers, Lijah. I don't want another car to drive over that section of highway before I get a good look. I'll be right there."

Chapter Three

Long before daylight the next morning, Ripp was sitting at his kitchen table wearing nothing but a pair of jeans and sipping his first cup of coffee. Outside, down the dirt road that ran past his property, a rooster was crowing and somewhere nearby he could hear Chester, his black Labrador, barking, probably at an armadillo that was determined to dig up the last of the potatoes in the vegetable garden.

Ripp had moved into the small, shotgun-style house five years ago, after his father, Owen McCleod, had lost a long battle with lung disease. The family farm, where Ripp and his older brother, Mac, had once helped their father raise corn and cotton, had held too many painful memories for both men. They'd sold the place and used most of the money to settle up the enormous medical bills that had piled up while their father fought to stay alive. As for their mother, Frankie, she'd left the family farm long ago, when her sons had been mere children of eight and ten years old. Neither Ripp nor his brother ever heard from the woman and both of them preferred it that way. She'd chosen another man over her husband and sons and neither of them had any use for her.

As for what money remained from the estate sale, Ripp had used his small amount to buy this two-acre spot on the outskirts of Goliad. The house was old and had needed lots of work when he'd purchased the property, but Ripp was handy with carpentry and he'd managed to do all the refurbishing himself. And even though the house was far from fancy, the results of his hard work never ceased to leave him with a sense of proud accomplishment. At night, when he walked through the door, he liked knowing that his home, his land, belonged to him rather than some downtown banker.

Across the small kitchen, atop a refrigerator so ancient it had rounded edges, a radio was spewing the local news and weather. However, Ripp was paying little attention to the information. Last night he'd gone to sleep with Lucita Sanchez on his mind and this morning when he'd opened his eyes she was right there again.

Lijah's discovery of the second set of tire marks had turned out to be correct, which meant that Lucita had been telling the truth. Someone *had* deliberately harassed her, then driven away from the scene after she'd crashed. The idea was more than disturbing to a man whose job was to keep the peace and ensure the safety of the citizens of the county.

Who did he think he was kidding? Ripp asked, as he

left the table to drop two pieces of bread into a chrome toaster. This wasn't about the citizens of Goliad County. This was something far more personal. Something about Matt's sister haunted him, riled him and even stirred his libido. For the first time since Pamela had broken their engagement four years ago, Ripp actually caught himself thinking of a woman in a sexual way and the realization shocked him.

The browned bread popped up with a loud snap. Ripp retrieved a container of butter and a jar of jelly from the refrigerator, spreading thick layers on both pieces before tossing them onto a saucer and eating both pieces while standing at the cabinet counter.

Okay, so he was still a red-blooded man after all, he thought as he dumped the crumbs into a waste basket. Looking at a woman and finding her attractive wasn't anything to get worried over. It only meant he'd returned to the land of the living. It didn't mean he was going to get involved with the woman. Hell's bells, that was a laughable notion anyway. Lucita Sanchez was as far away from his social circle as a woman could get.

Still, he couldn't let her continue to wonder if her recollection of the accident had been completely accurate. She had a right to know what had happened— and to know to be on her guard. But before Ripp let her know anything, he wanted to personally make an inspection of her car.

Glancing at the clock hanging on the opposite wall, he figured he had time to feed Chester, then jump into the shower and shave before he headed off to work. Hopefully, he'd have a few extra minutes to stop at Santee's before Sheriff Travers sent him off on a different matter.

An hour later, Ripp stood inside the chain-link fence surrounding Santee's salvage yard. Junior, the owner, had a special spot where he kept vehicles for the sheriff's department. The small area was locked away from the slew of public autos that found their way to his garage and salvage, so Ripp was quite certain that no one had tampered with Lucita's small red coupe since the accident.

That made his finding even more sinister as he squatted on his heels and stared at the busted area on the back bumper. Near the fracture were several streaks and residual chips of black paint.

Lucita had described the threatening vehicle behind her as black or dark-colored. She'd insisted the car had rammed her from behind and this damage confirmed that she'd been right.

His thoughts grim, Ripp walked back to his waiting truck. Once inside, he reached for the radio.

"Send Lijah over to Santee's with a crime scene kit. I'll be waiting here for him."

The dispatcher quickly advised Ripp that she understood the order and the radio went quiet as he hung the mike back on the dashboard.

Even though the morning was still early, he figured if Lucita felt well enough to work today, she was probably already on her way to St. Francis High School in Victoria.

Ripp hadn't taken down her telephone number. That wasn't normal procedure. Acquiring the offender's mailing address was the limit. And in spite of her being the sister of a close friend, he wasn't a man to break the rules. But now he had pertinent information regarding her accident.

Quickly, he picked up the cell phone lying on the console next to his seat and searched for the number for the Sanchez house. It rang twice before Juan, the family cook, answered.

"This is Deputy McCleod," he told the older man. "I need to speak to Matt. Has he left for work yet?"

"Wait. He might be gone. I'll go see."

Ripp could hear the clatter of the phone as the cook laid it down, then the noise of doors being opened and closed. Finally, after a couple of long minutes, faint voices sounded in the background, then boot steps grew closer and closer to the receiver.

"Matt here."

"Matt, I'm glad I caught you," Ripp told him. "Do you have a minute to talk?"

"Ripp! Sure I can talk. Is anything wrong?"

Of course he would think something was wrong, Ripp thought wryly. It was six in the morning. Not the usual time for a social call. "There could be," he admitted. "How is Lucita this morning?"

"I talked to her earlier this morning right after I got up. She's stiff and sore and has a little headache, but other than that she's fine. She was determined to go into school this morning. She just signed a new contract with St. Joseph back in June and classes started at the first of this month. She doesn't want to start missing days this soon on a new job. Are you calling to check on her or is this something about the accident?"

Since Ripp had driven Lucita home to the ranch, Matt must have assumed he'd taken a personal interest in his sister. The idea was a bit embarrassing, yet he couldn't deny that Lucita had sparked him with something more than official law business.

Feeling awkward now, Ripp said, "Uh—well, I'm glad to hear she's okay. But I have some news about her accident and I thought—I wanted to run it by you before I talked with her."

Matt was suddenly wary. "Why? What is it?"

"Last night after I left the ranch, Lijah and I scoured the whole scene from the point where Lucita's vehicle got into trouble to the spot where it actually left the highway. Your sister was right about someone following on her bumper, Matt. We discovered another set of skid marks."

There was a long pause as though he was trying to digest Ripp's revelation. "Are you sure?"

"Positive. And now I have something else to corroborate that evidence. I'm here at Santee's right now. I've just finished inspecting Lucita's car and I found damage on the back bumper. Black paint was left behind from contact with another vehicle."

Matt muttered harshly. "Damn. Damn. I figured Lucita was right about the whole thing. She's pretty levelheaded. So you haven't said anything to her about this yet?"

"Not yet." He paused as the memory of Lucita's face swam to the forefront of his mind. On the ride to the Sandbur, she'd been mostly quiet, her pretty features set in grim determination. He'd sensed there were all sorts of dark fears swimming around in her head and he'd desperately wanted to reassure her, to promise her that she had nothing to fear. But he couldn't make anyone those sorts of promises and he'd been left feeling frustrated and helpless. "Uh—last night I got the impression that your sister was a woman with a strong constitution, but this sort of news would shake anyone. I thought it might be better if this news came from you, Matt."

"Well, you're right about one thing—this shakes the hell out of me, Ripp. And it'll do worse to Lucita. I don't want her to know."

Ripp was so stunned he pulled the receiver away from his ear and stared at it as though he wasn't sure he'd heard his friend correctly.

"Matt! She has to know that someone was trying to harm her. The sheriff's department has to investigate this matter. In fact, Lijah is already on his way over here to gather evidence to send to the crime lab."

"Investigate all you need, Ripp. But why worry Lucita any more than she already is?" Matt countered. "There's not much we can do about it. Not unless you catch whoever it is. And I can't see that happening. Not unless he shows his face."

"Thanks for the vote of confidence, ole buddy," Ripp said tersely. "Guess you think all the sheriff's department does around here is sleep or pick up kids for throwing soda cans on the sidewalk."

"Hell, Ripp. You know that isn't what I mean!" Frustration was threaded through Matt's voice. "It's just that—this is my sister. And I can't see how paint on a bumper can tell you anything! If you ask me, it's got to be her ex. He always drove black, expensive sports cars. But if the Corpus police can't find him, I hardly think the Goliad County Sheriff's Department can!"

If anyone else had said these things to Ripp, he would be seeing red. But Matt was his friend. Probably his best friend. And he understood the man was frustrated and even frightened for his sister's safety.

Ripp looked over at Lucita's little red coupe. The front of the car was nothing more than crumpled fiberglass. He figured the only reasons she was still alive were the grace of God and the car's air bag. Just the thought of someone out there plotting to do harm to such a lovely slip of a woman burned Ripp with anger.

"So you believe it was her ex-husband who tried to run her down last night?" Ripp asked. "Why? What motive would he have for harming Lucita?"

"Who the hell knows? Derek Campbell is crazy. That's enough to worry me," Matt blurted hotly, then added more calmly, "I'm sorry if I sound unappreciative, Ripp. I know you'll do your best to get to the bottom of this. In the meantime I'll talk with Lucita. I'm sure she won't go along with the idea, but I'm going to try to talk her into letting the family hire a bodyguard for her. Or at least, in letting one of the wranglers drive her to and from work."

Ripp realized that trying to find the maniac who tried to run Lucita down would be like searching for one fire ant on an acre of pasture. Pretty nigh impossible. But he was a man who liked to beat the odds.

"That might not be a bad idea. In the meantime I'll ask around. Maybe somebody else was on the highway last night around the time of the incident. But that's unlikely. At that time of the evening, hardly anyone travels that stretch of highway." He reached for a pen. "You say Lucita's ex's name is Derek Campbell?"

"Right." Matt went on to give him the exact spelling before asking, "What are you going to do?"

"Search for any information I can gather about the man," he answered. The sound of an approaching vehicle had Ripp looking around just in time to see Lijah pulling into the salvage yard. "I gotta go, Matt. When you talk to Lucita you can also let her know that I'm dropping the reckless driving charges so she'll only have to deal with the speeding ticket."

"Well, I guess that's something positive, at least."

Remorse twisted Ripp's lips. Last night the man in him had simply wanted to take Lucita's statement as one hundred percent accurate, especially when she'd looked at him with those big brown eyes. But he was Sheriff Travers's chief deputy and he'd been forced to follow the rules.

"I'll let you know if I make any headway, Matt. And if Lucita encounters anything strange on the highway or receives any sort of threat, call me. Day or night. Hear?"

"God forbid, but if something else happens, you'll be the first to hear it, Ripp."

A week later, Lucita was in her classroom at St. Francis High School, cramming the last of her geometry papers to be graded into a nylon tote bag. The bell announcing the end of the last class had rung more than thirty minutes ago and she'd finally gotten her desk straightened and everything packed that she needed to take home.

The past week had been a trying one, with sporadic headaches and a slew of extracurricular activities after classes. Somehow she'd made it through without missing a day of work, but now she was totally exhausted. The only thing keeping her upright was the fact that it was Friday and she could hopefully catch up on sleep over the weekend.

Pausing at the open door of the principal's office, she waved a hand at the woman sitting behind the wide desk. "Have a good weekend, Maud."

The blond-haired principal gave her a weary smile. "You, too, Luci. And be sure and take care of that head."

Lucita absently touched a hand to the spot that her

cousin Nicci had stitched together. The gash was healing, but still terribly sore.

Her family had all been very upset about her accident. Matt had even been threatening to hire a private investigator and a bodyguard to watch over her. But she'd stood her ground. She didn't want anyone following her around as if she was some sort of celebrity or politician who needed to be guarded from the public. And she certainly didn't want a P.I. snooping into her privacy. She wanted to live like a normal person. Besides, she'd told them, it had probably been an angry student who'd simply been trying to scare her before the incident snowballed into an accident. Lucita wasn't sure she'd convinced any of them. After all, she wasn't entirely convinced, herself.

From what Matt had told her, Ripp had sent paint chips from her car's bumper to a crime lab in San Antonio. He was also searching for Derek's whereabouts. But since she and Matt hadn't heard from the deputy since then, it was evident he'd not found a substantial lead. Which wasn't surprising. For the past three years Derek had slipped off the radar. But Lucita wasn't going to dwell on her ex. He'd already ruined too much of her life. And why would he want to harm her now? He'd already gotten what he wanted—her money. He was a thief. Not a stalker.

Smiling at the principal, she said, "Don't worry. A couple of days of rest and I'll be like new."

With a final wave, Lucita moved on down the wide corridor leading to the front exit of the building. At this time of the day the halls of the Catholic high school were eerily quiet. Normally, Lucita loved being around groups of energetic teenagers. From the first day she'd entered the fourth-grade classroom where Mrs. Baldwin made learning an exciting venture for the whole class, Lucita had set her heart on being just like the feisty teacher. And that decision hadn't wavered as she'd grown into adulthood.

Even marrying Derek at twenty-two and giving birth to Marti three years later hadn't deterred her determination to get a degree in mathematics and her Texas teaching certificate. For the past twelve years she'd been teaching in a private school in Corpus Christi. The other teachers there had become like family to her. She'd hated to leave, but Matt had convinced her that with Derek gone and out of her life, there was no reason left for her and Marti to stay on the coast. Now she was starting over at St. Francis, trying to build new friendships and a new life and wondering if she'd done the right thing by coming home to the Sandbur.

Since her smashed car had gone to the graveyard at Santee's Salvage she'd been driving one of the ranch's work trucks. Matt and Cordero had tried to insist that she take one of their family cars, but she'd refused, reminding her brothers that she'd come home to the Sandbur to be with her family, not to use them. The brown Ford she'd collected from the ranch yard was several years old with ripped upholstery and a bed full of hay hooks, horse halters and fencing tools. Black decals of the S/S brand were plastered on both doors, leaving no doubt as to which teacher was driving the banged-up vehicle, but Lucita could care less about keeping up appearances. As long as she had transportation to and from work, she was content. As soon as her insurance policy settled, she'd find herself some little economical car that could make the sixty-plus-mile round-trip every day on a few dollars of gas.

This morning she'd managed to find a parking slot beneath one of the flowering pear trees growing at the edge of the school parking lot. Now as she opened the door and threw her tote bag and purse inside, she was glad for the shade. At least she could slide beneath the steering wheel without blistering her rear.

She'd started the engine and was about to jerk the floor shift into Reverse when she noticed a piece of folded notebook paper beneath her windshield wiper.

Probably a student who couldn't face her with some sort of request, she thought, or one who needed a second chance at a flunked test.

Sighing, she thrust the floor gearshift into Neutral and left the engine running while she stepped down to retrieve the paper. Once she was back in the truck, she started to toss the note into her purse and go on her way, but curiosity got the better of her at the last second and she unfolded the square.

The typed words in front of her were so unexpected and strange that for a moment she couldn't assimilate what she was reading. Then she began to shake.

Deposit one million dollars into this account by Wednesday noon. If you don't comply, you'll wish like hell you had. Derek

After the word *account* there was a row of numbers and the name of a nearby bank. As for the signature, since it was also typed, there was no absolute way to tell if her ex-husband had actually written it.

Oh, God. Oh, God. What was she supposed to do now?

Deputy McCleod. The tall, lanky lawman was the

first image to come to Lucita's frantically racing mind. Ripp had to know about this. Not just because he was the deputy working her case, but also because she trusted him. His solid presence would make her feel safe, something she desperately needed at the moment.

Lucita drove the twenty-six miles from Victoria to Goliad with her cell phone next to her on the seat and one eye on the rearview mirror. By the time she parked in front of the sheriff's department, she was still shaking, but she'd managed to gather her senses together. She walked into the building with gritty determination on her face.

"Can I help you?"

The question came from a female officer sitting behind a waist-high counter. She was much younger than Lucita, on the curvy side, with pale blond hair pulled into a ponytail.

"I'd like to speak with Deputy McCleod if he's here," Lucita told her.

The young officer's brows lifted marginally. "He's here. Just a minute."

The woman left the area behind the counter and disappeared down a corridor.

Lucita barely had time to glance around her surroundings before she heard returning footsteps. She looked around just as Deputy McCleod stepped into the foyer. From the look on his face, she was the last person he'd expected to see waiting on him.

"Lucita!"

Stepping forward, she offered him her hand. "Hello, Deputy."

Ripp took her hand, but rather than shaking it he found himself holding on to it tightly as he searched her face. Something was wrong, he decided. Her features were pinched and pale, her brown eyes glazed as though tears were close to the surface.

"Has something happened?"

"I—uh—sorta. I need to talk to you." She glanced at the other officer who was back behind the counter and watching the two of them with open curiosity. "Do you have a minute?"

Picking up on Lucita's wish to keep her issue private, he nodded. "Sure. I was on my way out anyway."

With his hand still holding hers, he led her out of the building and around to a side lawn where blooming crepe myrtle trees shaded two wrought-iron benches.

After he helped her onto one of the seats, he joined her. "We could have talked in my office. But with the jail being in the back of the building you sometimes hear things being yelled that you don't want to hear. This is more private. That was what you wanted, right?"

A faint blush crept across her cheeks and Ripp found himself smitten with the sight of her. She was wearing a sandy pink shirt with the collar flipped jauntily upward beneath a curtain of light brown hair. A matching straight skirt covered her slim hips and stopped just a fraction below her knees. When she crossed her shapely legs it was all Ripp could do to keep his eyes on her face.

"Actually, yes. I—something has happened and I figured you would want to know about it as quickly as possible."

Surprised, he stared at her. He'd talked to Matt earlier this morning and from what his friend had told him, there'd been no incidents regarding Lucita. Apparently, whatever this was had occurred in the past few hours. "What happened?"

Nodding, she reached for the handbag she'd placed at her feet. Ripp's gaze followed her movements, down the smooth line of her calf to the pointed black heels on her dainty feet. She was soft and petite and, for some reason that he didn't quite understand, made him extremely aware of his own masculinity.

Her expression sober, she answered. "I found this stuck beneath my windshield this evening when I was about to leave the school campus."

She handed him a piece of folded paper. Bemused, he opened it and scanned the brief sentences. The message left Ripp chilled to the center of his being.

Looking up at her, he stated the obvious. "Your ex-husband's name is Derek Campbell. This might not have anything to do with what's been going on, but just for clarification, did you drop his name?"

"While we were married I went by Lucita Sanchez Campbell. I dropped his name after the divorce. My son, Marti, goes by Sanchez and Campbell."

He glanced down at the paper in his hand and then back up to her face. Her deep brown eyes were dark pools reflecting fears and doubts that cut at him, filled him with a need to reach out to her.

"Do you think he wrote this? Is this something he might do to you?"

She looked frantic. "I—I don't know. I honestly don't think so. Not the man I married—though I suppose he could have changed. Still, anyone could have typed his name to that thing!"

She was right, of course. They needed more to go on than a piece of paper with typed words.

Hearing a thread of panic in her voice, he reached over and curled his fingers around her forearm. "Don't panic, Lucita," he said gently. "We're going to figure this out and catch whoever is threatening you."

"But what if this—this person tries to harm me or my son? And the money—I'm not a rich person. I mean, yes, the Saddler and the Sanchez families are rich—the ranch is rich—but personally I'm not. I—" Groaning helplessly, she shook her head. "Maybe I had better tell you everything."

Guardedly, he watched a cloud of shame wash over her face, an expression that surprised him almost as much as the note. He couldn't imagine a woman of her stature being ashamed of anything. "All right. Maybe you'd better," he said.

Those brown eyes turned to his again and the pleading light that flickered back at him had Ripp's fingers unconsciously tightening around her arm.

She sighed. "You were right the other night, Ripp. I was holding something back from you. Not about the accident—but it might have been pertinent information. I'm just not sure."

She'd called him Ripp, as though they actually knew each other, as though she considered him more than just a deputy. The notion filled him with a sense of importance, which was downright silly. It didn't matter what this woman thought of him personally. All he needed to concentrate on was helping her.

"Okay. So you didn't tell me everything. I'm listening now."

Behind them on a nearby street, light traffic was passing by. Above their heads, among the white blooms of the crepe myrtles, mockingbirds were squawking the announcement of sunset, yet the sounds hardly registered with Ripp. Everything inside him was waiting for her to speak.

"I have no idea where my ex-husband is," she said quietly. "He simply left three years ago—abandoned me without warning or a clue where he was going."

In Ripp's business he heard all sorts of stories, every imaginable kind of excuse and tale. Still, even though Matt had implied that Lucita's husband had disappeared, what he was hearing from her now totally stunned him. She wasn't the sort of woman that a man would simply abandon. She was a soft, beautiful lady. She was educated with an admirable career; she was someone with a prestigious family and rich heritage. What kind of man would walk away from that?

"I've got to admit I'm a little confused here, Lucita. When Matt spoke to me about his ex-brother-in-law, he didn't say anything about him abandoning you. You didn't know he was going to leave? Had you had arguments, threats, anything of that sort going on between the two of you?"

Her head bent, she muttered, "Nothing like that. Oh, we had arguments from time to time. Mostly over financial issues, but they were never violent. Just disagreements—like most married couples have. At the time I believed our marriage was solid. Then one evening Derek just never came home. I called the chemical company where he worked as an engineer—they hadn't seen him all day." She glanced up, her expression a picture of wry acceptance. "That was just the beginning. Shortly afterward I discovered he'd taken all my inheritance—the money that my parents had divided equally between us children. It was over a million dollars. Derek knew I rarely looked at that account, so he took advantage and withdrew it slowly so as not to alert me or the bank's attention."

This past week Ripp had learned from the Corpus police department that Derek Campbell was wanted for robbery. But he'd not realized the man had stolen a fortune—Lucita's fortune. "A hell of a thing," he murmured to himself as much as to her.

Her lips twisted into a bitter line. "He'd been my husband for ten years. I thought I knew him. I thought I could trust him. I had his name on all my savings accounts. That's the way a normal married couple does things, isn't it?"

She didn't wait for him to answer. Maybe she thought he couldn't answer such a question. Either way, she went on, her voice so tight it was hardly more than a reedy whisper.

"Since that day he vanished I haven't seen him. And I've only heard from him once, through the mail. About three months after he'd left, a letter arrived in the mail. It was postmarked from a little town in Southern Mexico."

Although Lucita had turned the letter over to the police as evidence, she'd not forgotten the contents. Derek had admitted he'd grown bored being a husband and father and was tired of pretending to be a happy family man. He'd wanted excitement in his life and said he understood that she and Marti needed love and security, something he was no longer capable of giving them. He apologized for taking the money, but he didn't feel guilty about it. After all, her family was wealthy; she could get more.

"So that was the only word you ever got from him? How did you acquire a divorce?"

She grimaced. "Along with the letter he'd sent a set of divorce papers, drawn up by a Corpus lawyer that he had used over the years. He'd already signed the document. All I had to do was take it to my personal lawyer to put the filing in motion." She paused and glanced away from him. "Putting my name at the bottom of the page was merely a formality. My marriage had been over long before that. I just hadn't known it."

Ripp wanted to tell her that she'd gotten rid of bad rubbish, but he kept the comment to himself. She'd already suffered enough without him reminding her that she'd made the mistake of marrying a loser.

Instead, he told her, "I talked with a detective from the Corpus Christi police. He said that Derek was wanted for robbery and that they'd tracked him as far as Laredo then lost his trail as he slipped over into Mexico. He says they have no current information indicating that the man might be back in the States."

"I'm not sure anyone is bothering to look," she said glumly. "My case is cold now. Besides, it wasn't a violent crime. Lawmen have more important cases to solve than a man disappearing with his wife's inheritance."

Ripp had to admit that what she was saying was true. Still, the idea that any man could have done something so heinous to this woman and her child left him sick.

"Lucita—before this happened—are you certain that this creep didn't give you some sort of clue to his intentions? I understand I'm getting pretty personal, but if Derek Campbell wrote this note, I need some clues to get into the guy's head before, God forbid, he makes his next move."

He watched her swallow hard. A part of him wanted

to move closer, to put his arm around her shoulder and comfort her. But she wasn't here seeking the comfort of a man, he reminded himself. She was here seeking the help of the law.

"We—uh, like I said before, our marriage had its ups and downs, but nothing out of the ordinary. Derek liked to have a good time and spend money. We sometimes quarreled about that. But he wasn't an abusive man. This threatening note—it seems totally out of character for him. But then I would have never guessed that the man was a greedy thief. If I had any inkling I would have safeguarded my Sandbur inheritance."

For any man to choose money over this woman was beyond Ripp's comprehension. But being a lawman, he knew firsthand that most crimes were centered on greed. It was a sad fact of life. "What about your son? Does he know about his father—about the money?"

She breathed deeply and he could see she was trying to collect herself. "I tried to keep most of the brutal facts from Marti, but after we came home to the Sandbur, he overheard Dad talking to me about the money. God, it was awful. Even though I'd warned him that Derek was never coming home, I think up to that point Marti wanted to believe that something had happened to his dad—that he was dead and couldn't return to us. You see, I'd never told my son about Derek's letter—how he'd written that he didn't want to be a husband or father anymore. But after that—well, Marti's had to face the fact that his own father didn't care about him or me. I worry about what that has done to him."

And what about her? Ripp wondered. After what this Campbell had done to her, how could she ever look at another man and trust him?

But she came to you, Ripp. She's putting her trust in you to help her. You can't let her down.

Emotions such as Ripp hadn't felt in a long time filled his throat and made his voice just a bit husky when he finally spoke.

"Maybe this note is the work of your husband, Lucita. Could be that he's back for more money. Right now we can only speculate. But I swear to you one way or the other, I'm going to find out who and what is behind this."

Something like hope flickered in her eyes and he was amazed at how special the sight of it made him feel.

"What are you going to do?" she asked.

He stood and pulled her up by the hand. "First we're going to hand this over to Sheriff Travers. If we're lucky, the crime lab will find prints on this paper that belong to someone other than you or me. Along with that we have a bank name and an account number. More than likely it was opened under a false identity, but even that might lead to someone. And then, after we see the sheriff, I'm going to follow you to the Sandbur and we're going to talk to your family about this."

She suddenly stuck her heels in the ground. "Wait, Ripp! I don't—I'd rather keep this mess from them. It will only worry everybody, and Marti is already upset."

Amazed that she still wanted to be so independent even in light of actual threats, he shook his head at her. "Marti won't have to hear about any of this. But the rest of your family deserves to know. The Sandbur has a prominent reputation. It's no secret that your family is rich. The person or persons behind this note are obviously after money. As far as we know, anyone close to you could be in danger, too."

Stricken by this thought, she whispered, "Oh, God, you're right. Marti or me might not be the only target here. Ripp, what am I going to do?"

This time Ripp didn't respond as a lawman to a citizen in need. Instead, he drew Lucita into the circle of his arms until her cheek was pressed against his chest and his hand was stroking down the long length of her hair.

"It's not what you're going to do, Lucita. It's what *I'm* going to do. And I promise I'm not going to let you down."

Chapter Four

Later that evening the living room of the Sanchez house was full of voices, the loudest belonging to Lucita's brother, Matt, who also happened to be the head ramrod of the Sandbur now that Geraldine Saddler was in semiretirement.

Pacing from one end of the room to the other, he punctuated each word by slashing his arm through the air. "The best thing Luci can do now is quit that damn job at St. Francis. There's no sense in her getting out on the highway and making herself a target for this predator."

Grateful that her aunt Geraldine had taken Marti out for the evening and away from the discussion of this worrisome turn of events, Lucita stared in dismay at her brother.

Juliet, Matt's wife, spoke up before Lucita had a

chance to utter any sort of protest. "Matt, can you hear yourself? Lucita has a life! She loves teaching just like you love what you do. Would you want someone demanding that you quit?"

Matt's brows arched. "That's a ridiculous comparison! Can't you understand that I don't want my sister killed?"

Juliet sighed and rolled her eyes toward the ceiling. Across from Lucita, her father, Mingo, leaned earnestly forward in his armchair.

He said, "Juliet is right, Matt. Luci can't hide herself away. What sort of life would that be for her?"

In another part of the room, sitting alone on a cowhide-covered love seat, Lex Saddler, Lucita's cousin and Matt's right-hand man, suddenly spoke up. "I agree with Matt. At the very least, I think Lucita needs to take a leave of absence from her job. We can keep an eye on her here at the ranch."

No longer able to keep quiet, Lucita rose to her feet and faced both men. "Leave of absence! Lex, I only signed my contract with St. Francis three months ago! I can't let the school down right off the bat!"

"You'd be more than letting them down if you let someone kill you!" Matt stormed at her.

While Juliet tried to calm her husband down, Lex said, "I'm sure if you make the school aware of the problem the administration will understand."

Behind Lucita, Ripp had been standing quietly near the fireplace hearth, but now he felt compelled to speak what was on his mind. "I don't think any of you have stopped to consider whether this danger might spill over onto Lucita's students. What sort of security system does St. Francis have, Lucita? Once you're at work, could an intruder get in?"

Not surprised that he would see a problem from all angles, Lucita turned to look at him. All this evening she'd felt his presence in the room and she'd felt calmed and supported by it. Strange that she should find more comfort in a man she hardly knew than in the protective relatives surrounding her.

"St. Francis has very tight security. It's located on the side of town that, unfortunately, has experienced gang violence, so once school starts the building is locked to outsiders, unless they can show valid identification and a pertinent reason for entering the school."

Ripp nodded in approval while Lex looked thoughtful. "Maybe Luci just touched on something. Could this note be from someone in one of these gangs? Someone that knows Luci is from a wealthy family?"

Ripp glanced at the other man. "It's sounds plausible, except for one thing—the note is signed 'Derek.' A gang member from Victoria wouldn't be privy to the name of Lucita's ex-husband."

Juliet wrapped her arm through her husband's as though the whole discussion was making her uneasy. "Perhaps Luci has a student named Derek. One that she's had trouble with. Have you, Luci?"

Lucita considered Juliet's question for several moments, then slowly shook her head. "I do have a Derek in an algebra I class, but he's a sweet child, a bookworm who's only interested in keeping his grades high enough to enter medical school someday. He wouldn't harm a rattlesnake even if it was about to bite him."

Rising from his armchair, Mingo addressed the whole gathering. "The way I see it, before we start trying to figure out who wrote the note, we need to figure out what we're going to do about it."

Lucita walked over to where her father stood. His stout, stocky figure was quite a contrast to what it had been only two years before when he'd been partially paralyzed and unable to speak. Thanks to God and a skillful neurosurgeon he was back to his robust self.

Yet now that Lucita had been threatened, she couldn't help but think about how her father's injury had been caused by a fight; an attack from two men that he'd never seen before. The offenders had never been caught, nor had the case been solved. Her father was a walking image of what happened when an enemy got too close. The whole notion dropped icy rocks to the pit of her stomach.

"What do you mean, Daddy?" she asked.

His big hand gently patted her cheek before he turned his attention to Ripp. "The demands. What are we supposed to do about depositing the million dollars? Put it there and see who draws it out? Wait?"

There was no doubt that the Sanchez family could easily produce a million dollars on their own without even having to draw in the Saddler family, Ripp realized. The Sandbur was worth millions many times over and to keep his daughter safe, Mingo would give up every penny he had. But Ripp understood that handing money over to an extortionist would never work.

"If we were one hundred percent certain that we could trace the money back to the perpetrator, I'd agree to setting him or her up and I'm sure Sheriff Travers would, too. But electronic withdrawals can sometime prove risky to follow. By the time we traced the electronic trail, the perpetrator could be long gone—with the million dollars."

"To hell with the million," Matt spoke up. "Money isn't the issue here. We—"

"Need to give in to this lunatic's demands?" Lex interrupted tersely. "You're crazy, Matt, if you think dropping a million will keep this idiot away from Luci. He'll only want more. If you ask me, that's exactly what's happened here. Derek has spent all the money he stole from Luci and now he wants more."

Matt glared at his cousin. "I didn't ask you, Lex, so butt out of this! Damn it, Luci is my sister and—"

Lex jumped to his feet and Lucita stared in horror as the words between the two men began to escalate into an all-out argument.

"Matt, if you think for one minute that you could love Luci more than me, then you're crazy. She's like my sister and don't you be telling me—"

"Shut up! Shut up, the both of you!" Lucita yelled at the two men. Before anyone could stop her, she ran from the room and kept running until she was out the back door and on the beaten path to the guesthouse.

Back in the living room, Mingo looked at Ripp. "Maybe you'd better go smooth her feathers," he suggested. "I don't think she's too happy with her family right now."

Ripp wasn't at all sure that he could lend Lucita much comfort, but everything in him wanted to try. From the moment the two of them had arrived on the Sandbur and her family had gathered around her in a smothering circle, he could sense she was close to collapsing.

"Yeah, Ripp," Matt spoke up in a remorseful voice. "Tell her we're sorry. I think we've all been too busy thinking about how we personally feel about the matter instead of considering Lucita's feelings."

Lex nodded with equal regret. "Matt's right. We ought to be helping her instead of making her feel more miserable."

"I'll see what I can do," Ripp told them, then hurried out of the room.

By the time he caught up to Lucita she was walking down a narrow stone walkway that led to the back of the guesthouse.

When he called her name, she turned and, with a faint frown on her face, waited for him to reach the spot where she stood next to a huge bougainvillea bush covered with scarlet-colored blooms.

Although the sun had long ago dipped behind the western horizon, there was still enough light left for him to clearly see her face. Tears had reddened her eyes and streaked her cheeks, but for the moment her crying had stopped and she studied him with faint annoyance.

"Why did you follow me? I want to be by myself."

Her voice was so strained it was little more than a painful rasp. Hearing it made Ripp want to step forward and pull her into his arms, press her cheek against his heart and simply hold her. The urge still felt odd to him. Especially since it had been years since he'd felt anything toward a woman.

"I'm sorry. Lex and Matt asked me to speak to you. They wanted me to apologize for their behavior."

"They couldn't speak for themselves?" she asked with sarcasm. "They sure weren't having any problems working their mouths a few moments ago."

A faint smile touched his mouth. "The guys only got steamed up because they care about you. You should be happy that you're loved that much."

The frown on her brow deepened as his words

tumbled through her mind and then without warning fresh tears brimmed onto her cheeks.

"Oh, Ripp—I realize they care. But I can't take this! I don't know what's happening—what will happen! I want answers, not arguing about the best route to get them!" She paused long enough to swallow and wipe at the tears on her cheeks. "I think—I've made a terrible mistake by coming home to the Sandbur. Now I've put everyone in danger."

"You're talking foolish now. This is the time that you need your family around you. If this had to happen, at least it happened here, where you won't be alone."

The quiet firmness of his words broke through her chaotic emotions and as she looked at him as her shoulders slumped in surrender. "You're right. But I just can't take any more of their bickering this evening." With a weary sigh, she looked toward the guesthouse then back to him. "Would you care to come in for a cup of coffee or a glass of iced tea?"

The invitation surprised Ripp. Though he told himself it was nothing personal, he couldn't help but take it that way. "I wouldn't want to put you out," he said.

She gave him a wan smile. "After all I've put you through this evening, a little refreshment is nothing."

"All right," he told her. "I could sure use a cup of coffee."

"Good. Just follow me."

She opened a back door to the house and they entered a mudroom equipped with a double sink and industrial-sized washer and dryer. Cowboy boots and tennis shoes, along with other odds and ends, lined one wall, while a pile of dirty laundry was waiting to be loaded into the washer.

Beyond the mudroom was the kitchen and once Lucita had turned on an overhead fluorescent light, she gestured for Ripp to have a seat at a long wooden farm table covered with a navy-and-white checked cloth. The small bouquet of fresh blue cornflowers and pink sweet peas sitting in the middle instantly reminded Ripp of how different this kitchen was from his own. And the difference was more than just the modern appliances and the intricately carved oak cabinets. The room had a woman's touch, a softness that his had never seen.

Definitely feeling out of place, he took a seat at the end of the table, then pulled off his Stetson and placed it, crown down, on the floor next to his chair. While he raked fingers through his flattened hair, he watched Lucita fill a coffee carafe with water.

She'd not taken the time to change her clothes since they'd arrived at the Sandbur and Ripp was secretly glad. If he looked at her for days in that sexy pink skirt, it still wouldn't be long enough. Like a clinging hand, the fabric hugged the shape of her hips and gentle slope of her thighs. She was classy and gorgeous in an understated way. The sort of woman that could have most any man she wanted. Yet she was alone....

"Do you like living here in the guesthouse?" he asked, mainly as a way to quiet his roaming thoughts.

"I do. When I finally decided to come home, Matt wanted me to move into the big house with the rest of the family. But with his brood growing and Cordero and Anne-Marie living there periodically with their baby son, I didn't want to make the house more crowded. Besides," she added as she glanced over her shoulder at him. "I like my privacy. Marti and I are used to being alone."

Ripp hadn't yet met her son, but he could tell from

the tone of her voice and the softening of her features when she spoke of him that she loved the boy very much. Which was hardly a surprise. He didn't have to ask; one look into Lucita's gentle eyes had told him she was a person who loved others, rather than herself. She was the sort of woman who would put the safety and happiness of her child and her family before her very life, a quality that made Ripp even more concerned about her welfare.

"I can't imagine what all of this has done to your son—losing his father in such a way."

With the basket of ground coffee shoved in place, Lucita switched on the machine and walked over to where Ripp sat.

Having a man, especially one that looked like Ripp McCleod, in the kitchen was jarring to her senses. True, she was used to being around tough, brawny cowboys here on the ranch, but there was something more to this lawman that made her skin prickle and her heart beat far too fast.

Sighing, she pulled out the chair kitty-corner from him and sank gratefully onto the seat. "Time has helped soften the blow, but Marti's not the same boy. Oh, he still smiles and laughs and does the normal things that boys his age like to do, but underneath I can tell that he's confused and hurting." Her eyes shadowed with unknown fears, she looked across the corner of the table and met Ripp's blue eyes. "If something comes of this extortion note, I'm scared to think of how it might affect him."

He shook his head and Lucita's gaze was drawn to the thick hank of hair falling over the right side of his forehead and tumbling in unruly waves around his ears. The color was a rich blend of chocolate and copper and the strands glistened like the coat of Matt's prize stallion. On the whole he was damned attractive. More than a man should have the right to be. And, though it was a stupid time for her mind to be straying, she couldn't help but wonder if he'd ever been married or had a special woman in his life.

His voice broke into her unbridled thoughts. "Don't put the cart before the horse, Lucita. This could be just someone wanting to scare you—to make your life miserable."

Her lips compressed to a tight line. "They're doing a darn good job of it." Glancing over her shoulder, she could see the carafe was full of coffee. Quickly excusing herself, she went over to the cabinet and began to fill two yellow mugs with the hot brew.

"Cream or sugar?" she asked.

"No. Just plain will be fine."

As she carried the drinks to the table, Ripp's cell phone emitted a muffled ring from his shirt pocket.

After quickly flipping it open, he announced, "It's Sheriff Travers, I'd better answer it."

Lucita sank back into her seat and waited awkwardly for him to finish the brief conversation.

"Right. I think I should. I'll tell her that," he finally concluded.

Sensing the conversation pertained to her, Lucita hardly waited for him to end the call before she urgently asked, "What? Does the sheriff have new information regarding the note?"

Ripp frowned. "He's verified that there is such an account number at the bank, but apparently the name and address given are phony."

Lucita visibly wilted. "How could that be, Ripp?

Wouldn't the person that opened the account have to show identification?"

"Sure. But phony documents are easily obtained for the right price, from the right people."

Feeling as though someone had whacked the oxygen from her lungs, she wiped a weary hand across her forehead. "So what does this tell us, if anything?"

"Well, we know that the account is listed as belonging to a female."

Lucita stared wide-eyed at him, wanting to feel relief, but afraid to. "Female! Then it wasn't Derek?"

Ripp's expression was patiently indulgent. "We can't assume that the woman worked alone. Could be Derek is connected to her."

After a moment's consideration, she nodded glumly. "It's obvious that I don't have investigating skills. Even if I do teach math, I can't think of those types of angles."

"Your line of work isn't trying to think ahead of a criminal." His expression thoughtful, he lifted the mug to his lips and took a careful sip. "Sheriff Travers sent another deputy over to the bank to interview the employee that supposedly opened the account. According to her, the person was a female with blond hair, but she couldn't be sure. With all the faces that pass through the bank each week, the employee's memory was fuzzy, to say the least."

Lucita wanted to weep, but she wouldn't allow herself the luxury. She'd already broken down once in front of this man. She didn't want him to get the idea that her backbone crumbled every time she was faced with a personal trauma.

"I don't want to be negative about this, Ripp, but none of this information sounds as though it will help."

"It's a start. Most crimes aren't solved instantly. They're done bit by bit with pieces of information that alone look worthless, but together form a picture."

Just having him talk, hearing the quiet confidence in his voice helped soothe her. Leaning back in her chair, she regarded him with an interest she couldn't hide.

"You like what you do, don't you?"

With a wry grin, he replied, "I can't imagine doing anything else. My father was Owen McCleod. Maybe you remember him—he was the sheriff of Goliad County for over fifteen years."

"Owen McCleod," she repeated thoughtfully. "Yes, I believe I do remember him. Wasn't he the sheriff who had that shoot-out on Main Street with a pair of bank robbers?"

Fond remembrance marked Ripp's features as he nodded. "That was my father. He took a bullet to the shoulder during that little scuffle. The robbers ended up getting forty years apiece."

"I'm impressed. And I'm sorry I didn't connect your name with his before now."

His low chuckle was full of modesty. "Don't put me in the same league as my father. He was an iron man. Everyone respected him."

"Was?"

He glanced away from her but not before Lucita saw his blue eyes fill with loss.

"Yeah. He died about five years ago—a bad case of emphysema. After that my brother and I sold the farm. It just wasn't the same hanging around the place after Dad was gone."

"Farm?" She frowned. "Your father was a sheriff. How did he have time to farm, too?"

Ripp turned his gaze back on her. "Farming was

earlier in his life. While us boys were still young we raised corn and cotton. But the year I graduated high school we had a particularly hard drought and we nearly went under financially. That's when a friend talked Dad into running for sheriff. After that, being a lawman became his life. And I guess it seeped over into his sons' blood. My brother, Mac, is a deputy, too, over in Bee County."

Curious, she asked, "Your mother didn't want to keep the farm?"

His jaw hardened and when he spoke Lucita couldn't miss the bitterness in his voice.

"She didn't have any say in the matter. She's been gone from here for a long, long time—since Mac and I were kids."

Something had gone very wrong with his parents' marriage, but Lucita wasn't going to ask him any more. That sort of information needed to be given voluntarily, not pried out with a shovel.

"I'm sorry for that," she said softly, then purposely tried to brighten the moment with a smile. "So both you and your brother are in law enforcement. Do you have other siblings besides Mac?"

Staring into the contents of his cup, he murmured, "No. It's just Mac and me. He's thirty-nine, a little more than a year older than me."

In spite of her own problems, Lucita could feel herself being drawn more and more into Ripp's life. And though it might not be wise, she was glad for the distraction, glad that he was here to divert her attention from the note she'd pulled from beneath her windshield wiper. "Does Mac have a family?"

A wry smile curved the corner of his lips. "Mac was

married once, but that ended after a couple of years. He's not looking to make a second attempt at having a family."

Her heart beating even more swiftly, her forefinger unwittingly drew imaginary patterns on the side of her coffee mug. "And what about you, Ripp? Do you have a family?"

His eyes briefly connected with hers before settling on a row of windows that looked out on the back lawn.

"No. I came close to having a wife once. But that…didn't work out."

Even before she'd asked the question, a feeling deep within had whispered to Lucita that he wasn't a family man. He might have a lover, but she felt sure he wasn't a man who woke up with the same woman next to him every morning.

A faint flush of pink colored her cheeks and she quickly glanced away from him. "Well, I try to believe that everything happens for the best. And look at me. At least you're not going through something like this."

"You didn't ask for this sort of trouble. And it would be narrow-minded of you—of any of us—to point the finger at your ex-husband."

She turned her gaze back to him and the sincerity she saw on his face punctured a hole in the dark cloak she hid her private life behind. Before she could stop them, things were tumbling out of her mouth that she normally didn't speak to anyone, even her own family.

"You're right. I guess my mind keeps turning to him because—well, he's the only person who's ever intentionally hurt me."

"And now you feel foolish for ever trusting him."

Surprised that he understood, she looked at him and wondered if his own broken relationship had left him feeling the same way. "When I first started dating Derek in college, Daddy tried his best to warn me about him. Mingo saw Derek as a parasite, a man after my money. I refused to listen to his warnings. Instead, I chose to believe Derek's charming lies." With a heavy sigh, she rose from the chair and walked over to the windows looking out over the backyard. Staring bleakly out at the darkening evening, she said, "What gets me the most, Ripp, is that I was deceived for so long. For ten years I thought my husband loved me. To discover that he didn't—it was like having my feet knocked from under me."

Long moments passed as quietness settled over the room. Lucita figured she had embarrassed the deputy by revealing so much about her personal life. She was about to turn and apologize when she felt his hand suddenly on her back.

His touch was warm and solid and she had the strangest urge to lean against his chest, to invite his arms to circle around her.

"Whether your ex had anything to do with the note is beside the point. He deserves to be locked away, Lucita. And I aim to see that he is."

Tears suddenly scalded her throat and she had to swallow several times before she could turn to face him.

"Oh, Ripp, I—" Tilting her head back, she rested her palms in the middle of his broad chest. "I—"

Finding it impossible to put her feelings in words, she rose on her tiptoes and touched her lips softly to his.

By the time Ripp realized she was kissing him, the

back door to the kitchen burst open. Lucita jerked away from him just before Marti rounded the corner.

The boy stood staring at his mother standing next to a man with a gun on his hip.

Chapter Five

Though dazed by the sudden interruption, Lucita still leaped away from Ripp and smiled as brightly as she could at her son.

"What's he doing here?" Marti asked with child-like candor.

Lucita opened her mouth to explain, but before she could get a word out, Ripp walked over to the tall, slender boy with a face full of freckles and a wary look in his gray eyes.

Extending his hand to Lucita's son, Ripp introduced himself, "Hello, young man. I'm Ripp McCleod. A deputy for Goliad County."

Still obviously rattled to find a man in the house, particularly a lawman, Marti turned one eye toward his mother while he shook hands with Ripp.

"Mr. McCleod is Sheriff Travers's chief deputy,

Marti," Lucita explained, then glanced uncertainly up at Ripp. "And—uh, he came by the ranch this evening because—"

Sensing her unease, Ripp quickly intervened. "I was the officer who reported your mother's car accident the other night. I came by this evening to deliver some papers to her that she needed for her insurance."

Ripp wasn't normally a fibber, but in this case, he understood that Lucita needed time to decide how and what to explain to Marti about the extortion note. Whether she decided to let her son know about the threat was her own personal business, not his or the sheriff's department.

The boy's face relaxed. "Oh. That's good. I mean, I thought somebody here on the ranch had done something wrong. I'm glad it was just some old paper stuff."

Ruffling the top of Marti's reddish-brown hair, Lucita did her best to let out a casual chuckle. "You can relax, son. Deputies don't arrest kids for not doing their homework."

Lucita exchanged another quick glance with Ripp and he could see the relief in her eyes. He could also see that Marti had equated his presence with someone doing something wrong instead of a response to an accident. No doubt, Derek Campbell's behavior had affected the boy in a multitude of negative ways, he thought regretfully. Just as his mother's abandonment had carved painful nicks in his own life.

Rolling his eyes, Marti groaned. "Oh, Mom, you're gonna have Deputy McCleod thinkin' I'm a little kid. I'm going on twelve years old! That's almost a teenager!"

Sharing an indulgent smile with Ripp, she reminded her son, "You won't be twelve for eight more months."

"Well, Aunt Geraldine says the next eight months will just fly by," he reasoned.

"I'm sure they will," Lucita agreed.

"Does something special happen when you're twelve?" Ripp asked him.

The boy, who was tall for his age, drew himself even taller as he looked at Ripp. "My grandpa is goin' to let me have a really great horse. One that I can cut on—like my cousin Gracia. She has all sorts of cool ribbons and trophies and medals that she's won in competition. And she says that I can be as good as her. She and grandpa are goin' to teach me."

"Gracia is Matt's daughter," Lucita explained to Ripp. "Since you're friends with Matt and my father, I'm sure you've met her before."

Obviously she didn't remember him from those years ago when he'd been in high school with her brother Matt. But he could hardly fault her for that. Ripp had been older than her and since he and Matt had only palled around at school and a few places in town, she'd never seen him on the Sandbur or been properly introduced to him.

"Yeah, I became acquainted with Gracia right after she was born. Matt and I go way back—we were buddies in high school." Turning to Marti, he asked, "You like to ride horses?"

The boy gave him a short nod. "Yeah. A lot. I didn't get to do it much when we lived in Corpus. But now that we live here on the ranch I get to ride all the time. But—" frowning, he looked accusingly at his mother "—Grandpa makes me ride nags, 'cause Mom's afraid I'll fall off and get hurt."

"Trampus isn't a nag," Lucita gently scolded. "He's devoted to you and has willingly taken you for miles over this ranch. What do you plan to do when you get this new horse, just forget him because he's old? That's not the way anyone treats a true buddy."

It was obvious from the sheepish look on Marti's face that his mother's gentle reproach had left him a little ashamed of himself.

"Aww, Mom, I ain't gonna do Trampus that way." Turning his attention on Ripp, the boy suddenly changed the subject. "Deputy McCleod, you have a funny name—Ripp. Who gave it to you?"

Ripp chuckled. "I was named after my grandfather Ripley McCleod. But my father shortened it to Ripp. You can call me that, if you like."

"Oh. Guess that makes sense," he said, then with a thoughtful frown asked, "Ripp, have you ever drawn your gun on anybody?"

"Only twice in more than ten years. It's not something a lawman does lightly. We have to have a very serious reason for drawing our firearm."

"Yeah. Guess you would," he said, then scuffing the toe of his tennis shoe against the tile floor, he glanced uncomfortably away from Ripp. "You ever arrest anybody for stealing things—like money?"

Ripp couldn't count the times that he'd had to watch good people and good families see their loved one carted away in handcuffs. It was never a pleasant sight. But knowing what was going through Marti's head right at this moment was somehow even worse. Ripp might not have had a mother, especially a loving mother like Lucita was to Marti, but he'd had a great father. He couldn't imagine how this boy must feel to know that his father was a thief. Even worse, a thief who didn't care one iota about his own son.

"Sometimes, I do."

Marti's mouth tightened as he continued to avoid Ripp's gaze. "Well, I guess they deserve it."

Ripp glanced at Lucita to see her face had taken on a soberness that cut right through to a soft spot in his heart.

"That's something the courts have to decide, Marti," Ripp told him.

Lucita suddenly cleared her throat. "Son, it's getting late. You'd better feed the cat and do your homework."

"Okay," he mumbled, then politely reached to shake hands again with Ripp. "It was nice meetin' you, Ripp McCleod."

"Same here, Marti. Maybe we'll see each other again sometime."

Marti shrugged as though he very much doubted that would happen. "Yeah, sure."

Lucita sighed as he turned and trotted toward the mudroom. Once her son was completely out of sight, she looked gratefully at Ripp. "Thank you for coming to my rescue," she said in a hushed voice. "I hadn't been expecting Marti to come home this early."

One corner of Ripp's mouth turned upward. "And find a lawman in his mother's kitchen?"

She could feel warm color seeping into her cheeks. He made it sound as though his being here had very little to do with him being a deputy. And maybe he was right. She hadn't necessarily invited him in because he wore a badge on his chest and a gun on his hip. She'd simply wanted to spend a few more minutes with the man. What could that mean? That this whole thing was turning her common sense upside down?

There was no question about that. She'd kissed the man! Dear God, what could he be thinking?

"Well, I'm sure the sight of you in your uniform was a little intimidating."

The search of his blue eyes touched her face like fingertips exploring in the dark. The sensation left her slightly breathless.

"I think his first impression was that I was here because of his father. Does he want Derek to be found? Prosecuted?"

Letting out a long, pent-up breath, she wiped a palm across her forehead. He wasn't going to mention the kiss. He was going to dismiss the whole thing. She wasn't sure how she felt about that. "I'm not sure. He says that as far as he's concerned, his father is dead."

"I'm sorry, Lucita," he said gently. "I imagine the whole thing is easier for him to deal with that way."

Too stung with emotions to make any sort of reply, she nodded, then walked back over to the table and picked up their coffee cups. "Our coffee has gotten cold," she said huskily. "Would you like more?"

"No. It's getting late and I have chores waiting on me at home. I'd better not keep you any longer."

She placed the cups on the cabinet counter while he retrieved his hat from the floor by his chair. But once he started toward the door, she couldn't stop herself from following.

"Thank you, Ripp, for being here for me and my family. I—we all appreciate your concern."

His hand on the doorknob, he paused to glance over his shoulder at her, and Lucita's heart melted just a fraction as she watched his features soften.

"You'll get through this, Lucita. We all will."

"Good night, Ripp."

Nodding, he slipped out the door. Lucita stood where she was and tried to regain her breath.

She'd kissed him. Not just a peck on the cheek. She'd kissed his lips. Purposely, gently, sweetly. Driving down the narrow asphalt road to his farmhouse, Ripp couldn't stop himself from recalling how Lucita's small hands had pressed themselves against the center of his chest, how her face had tilted up toward his. Almost as though she'd wanted him to take her into his arms. Had she? Or was his wishful imagination running wild with him?

Hell, Ripp, you're not a naive teenager anymore, he inwardly scolded himself. *You know the sorts of games that women play with men.*

The corners of his mouth turned bitterly downward. Yeah, he knew, all right. After three long years of thinking he'd found a woman who'd stick by his side, Pamela had shown him her true colors. When she walked away with another man, his pride had suffered some mighty deep wounds and so had his trust in women.

Still, Lucita didn't seem the sort of woman who would play a flirting game, he argued. No, she'd already been too hurt herself to tease or entice without reason. So what had she been doing?

Trying to thank you, Ripp. That's all. Forget it. Forget her.

Ripp was still mentally chiding himself when he turned a short curve and his house appeared a hundred yards ahead of him. Lights were shining through the living room window, and in the front, parked beneath a huge pecan tree, was his brother's shiny black pickup truck with the Beeville County Sheriff's Department emblem plastered on the side. Apparently, Mac had wandered out of his jurisdiction for some official reason; otherwise he'd be driving his own personal vehicle.

In front of the yard fence, Ripp shoved his own truck into Park and hurried inside.

He found Mac sitting on the couch in front of a small television set. On the coffee table was an open pizza box with more than half of the contents remaining.

"Hey, brother, come on in and make yourself at home," Mac greeted with a lazy grin.

"Hey, yourself. What are you doing here?" Ripp asked as he unbuckled his holster and placed the weapon on a nearby rolltop desk.

Mac, who most folks said resembled their father, was taller than Ripp and a bit stockier in build. His black hair had begun to frost just a tad near his side-burns, but his glinting smile said he was still very young at heart.

"I thought I'd have supper with my brother, but it seems he's been out gallivanting all over the county. I was about to give up on you and take the rest of this pizza home. I kinda like it for breakfast, too. Besides, I'm all out of eggs. Have the hens been laying?"

Mac wasn't a farmer. He'd never liked it even when their father had made a living working the land. Once he'd taken up being a deputy, Mac had completely forsaken turning soil or feeding livestock. Ripp, on the other hand, still liked keeping animals and chickens around the place and raising a patch of vegetables in the summer.

"Well, some of us have to work for a living," Ripp replied. "And, yes, the hens are laying. Remind me before you leave and I'll get you a couple of dozen eggs."

Leaving the room, he went to a bathroom and

quickly freshened up before returning to his brother's company. Mac had moved to the kitchen where he was heating a few slices of the pizza in the microwave.

"I thought you'd like it better hot," he said when Ripp entered the room.

Ripp shook his head with wry amazement. "My brother being thoughtful? What's come over you?"

Mac chuckled as the microwave dinged and he pulled out the plate of pizza. "I'm not always lazy and selfish."

He placed the plate on the kitchen table and gestured for Ripp to take a seat. "Eat. I'll get you something to drink." He walked over to the refrigerator and looked inside. "What do you want?"

"Give me the same thing you drank," Ripp told him.

Mac fetched a longneck beer from the refrigerator and placed it in front of his brother. After that he pulled out a chair and sat opposite of Ripp.

"So what are you doing out of Bee County?" Ripp asked him.

"I came over to collect a prisoner. You guys locked him up the first of the week for drunken assault, but we had warrants on him for burglaries."

"Obviously something happened and you didn't pick him up."

Mac shook his head. "Something about the court papers weren't completed. Guess I'll have to make another run on Monday. But that's all right—he'll be cooling his heels in jail no matter if he's in your county or mine."

Ripp nodded as he gobbled down the first slice of pizza. He'd been so wrapped up in Lucita and that damned extortion note that he just now remembered he'd not eaten since eleven o'clock this morning.

"So what have you been up to? I haven't seen you for a couple of weeks." Even though Ripp was very close to his brother, days could go by without the two of them calling or seeing one another. Yet that didn't mean they weren't thinking about each other. In that aspect, the two of them were almost like twins.

Mac leaned back in the wooden chair and propped his ankle against his knee. "Same old thing. Work, eat and sleep. What about you? Anything going on around here?"

Ripp reached for another slice of pizza. "Yeah. A hell of a lot. I just drove in from the Sandbur ranch. Matt's younger sister, Lucita, is being threatened."

Wide-eyed with interest, Mac leaned forward. "Lucita! I didn't know she was living around here now. I heard she was living in Corpus Christi."

Ripp looked at him while trying not to feel prickly. "I wasn't aware that you knew the woman."

Mac's chuckle was suggestive enough to put a scowl on Ripp's face.

"I don't know her personally, but I remember seeing her in high school. She was quite a looker. Don't tell me that you didn't remember her! Matt was your best friend, you ought to have known her!"

Frowning, Ripp said, "Matt and I were both older than Lucita. And I never hung around the Sandbur back in those days before she left the area. Besides, I wasn't girl crazy like you, big brother. While I was in high school I had learning on my mind, not chasing skirts."

Mac let out a hoop of laughter. "Yeah. Right. That's a real funny one, Ripp."

"Well, nothing is funny about what's going on now. She was involved in a deliberate hit-and-run a few nights ago.

Today she found an extortion note pinned beneath the windshield wiper on her vehicle. This person wants a million dollars deposited into a certain bank account or else something bad is going to happen to her or her family."

Mac's face instantly sobered. "Got any ideas who might be involved?"

"Her ex-husband's name was typed at the end of the note, but Sheriff Travers isn't at all convinced that it's him. I'm not so sure, either."

Ripp could see the wheels in his brother's head start to turn.

"So she's divorced," Mac mused aloud. "Sounds like a typical case of stalking an ex to me. Especially when the ex is rich. I'm surprised this thug didn't ask for more than a million."

Ripp quickly explained the circumstance of Lucita's divorce and ended with the impact the whole thing had had on Marti.

"I don't know, Mac," Ripp went on with a thoughtful frown. "Travers may be right. Derek is almost too obvious a suspect here. The more I think about it, the more I think it's someone wanting everyone to blame this creep."

As Ripp continued to eat, Mac didn't make an immediate reply. But after a few moments he leaned back in his chair and leveled a keen gaze on his brother.

"I'll tell you what I think. You've already gotten too close to this case. And if you don't step back and take a deep, mind-clearing breath you're gonna wind up getting hurt."

Annoyed now, Ripp rose from his chair and crossed over to the counter. As he shoved the coffeemaker's carafe under the faucet and turned on the water, he said tersely, "Don't be warning me about getting personal. Hell, you and I both know we wouldn't be worth a damn at our jobs if we didn't care."

Shutting off the water, he looked pointedly over his shoulder at Mac. "Maybe you've forgotten about the time you got so personally involved with the little boy who'd been abused that you wanted to adopt him yourself. You were devastated when the court finally handed him over to his grandparents."

The other man grimaced. "That's a hell of a thing to bring up. You're hitting below the belt now, Ripp."

"Sorry. I don't mean to rub salt in an old wound. I'm just pointing out—well, standing back and looking at everything from a distance is damn hard to do."

Mac's lips twisted wryly. "Especially with a woman like Lucita?"

Ripp turned his attention back to putting the coffee makings together. "That's a nasty thing to say. Especially when you know that Matt has been my best friend for years."

"That doesn't make Lucita any less beautiful."

Ripp turned another frown on his brother. "How do you know she's beautiful? You didn't even know she was living back on the Sandbur."

Mac's grin turned sly. "No. I didn't know where she was. But I know that women like her don't change."

Ripp bristled even though he realized it was stupid to let his brother's words get to him. Lucita didn't belong to him. She never would, so it was damned ridiculous of him to be feeling this possessive of a woman who'd merely kissed him.

"What's that supposed to mean?" he asked guardedly.

Mac shrugged. "Just that her type—well, they're born with class. Nothing, not even the passing years, can change that."

Yeah, she was classy all right, Ripp thought. She was classed right out of his league. His brain understood that, but it couldn't convince the man in him to forget her.

Chapter Six

Ripp. Even though Lucita hadn't seen the sexy deputy since she'd kissed him last Friday evening in the kitchen, the man continued to dwell in her thoughts.

In the past five days, she'd spoken to him twice on the phone. He'd called to update her on the investigation of the extortion note, but even the seriousness of the situation hadn't stopped her mind from wandering to the low, husky lilt of his voice and envisioning his strong face.

You're losing it, Lucita. Now isn't the time to be thinking about a man in that sort of way. There will never be a time. Unless you want to put your heart on the chopping block again.

With a weary sigh, Lucita hefted the duffel bag filled with work she was taking home and left the St. Francis building. For the past two days since she'd returned to work, a wrangler had followed her from the Sandbur all the way to school in the morning and would reappear when it was time for her to make the trip home.

This evening as she made her way across the parking lot, she expected to see one of the ranch's work trucks parked behind hers. Instead, she saw a black truck with the Goliad Sheriff's Department emblem on the side.

Instantly, her heart kicked into overdrive. Was it Ripp? Had something happened on the ranch?

Hurrying across the blistering asphalt, she reached the truck just as Ripp's tall figure stepped to the ground.

"Ripp, what's wrong?" she asked frantically before he could get a word out. "Is Marti okay?"

The fear she was feeling must have been mirrored on her face. He quickly clasped a steadying hand on her shoulder and the warmth from his fingers spread like a calming drug through her veins.

"He's fine. He's already home from school and staying with Gracia. Sorry the sight of me scared you. I should have called and let you know that I'd be here this evening to see that you get home safely."

She frowned with puzzlement. "What about Frank?"

He looked at her blankly and she hurriedly explained, "The wrangler who's been following me home."

"Matt agreed that it would be better for me to be here this evening," he replied.

Because today was Wednesday and the extortion note had demanded the money be deposited by that time. She and the rest of the family had chosen not to give in to the note writer's demands. Now there was nothing left to do but wait and see if there would be any sort of retaliation. But even that chilling reminder wasn't enough to dim her joy at seeing him again.

Just standing next to him left her feeling as though she was floating on a cloud. She couldn't stop a smile from spreading across her face. "Thank you for being here. I realize this must be eating into your regular duties."

His eyes met hers as a faint grin touched his face. "Your case has become my regular duties." His hand slid from her shoulder to cup her elbow. "Are you ready to leave? I'm not keen on you standing out here in the open like this."

To emphasize his concern, he took a moment to inspect the open area around them. Lucita was instantly reminded that she could be a target and that this tough deputy wasn't here on a social call.

Determined not to show an ounce of fear, she straightened her shoulders and gave him a smile.

"Sure. I'm ready."

He followed her over to the truck she'd been driving since her car had been laid to rest at Santee's, but before she could open the truck door, Ripp pulled her to one side.

"Wait. I just drove up a minute ago. I haven't had time to make sure no one has tampered with your vehicle."

Lucita couldn't believe he was taking the time to look under the hood and beneath the carriage. The whole thing was like something out of an espionage movie and a bad one at that, she thought, as he finally turned back to her.

"Everything looks clean."

"Is all of this really necessary, Ripp? I mean, why would anyone try to sabotage my vehicle? If I'm dead, they won't have a chance of getting money from me," she reasoned.

He helped her into the cab.

"Think of it this way, Lucita, if something happened to you, the remainder of your family would be so scared they'd probably be glad to hand over millions to this idiot to protect Marti. That's the way a criminal mind works."

There was logic to his thinking, even if the precautions he was taking seemed surreal.

"I suppose you're right," she admitted. "But I don't like this, Ripp. I want it to be over."

His features softened and Lucita had to believe he was looking at her purely as a man. The compassion she saw in his blue eyes was more than a deputy concerned for a county citizen.

"I want it to be over for you, too," he said gently.

Feeling awkward now, she nodded and reached for her seat belt. He waited to see that she'd carefully strapped herself in before he patted the side of the truck door.

"Drive carefully," he ordered, his voice returning to a brisk businesslike tone. "I'll be right behind you. If we're separated by traffic lights, slow down until I can catch up with you. Okay?"

With another jerky nod of her head, she said, "If that happens, I'll pull over and wait."

Thankfully, the thirty-five-minute drive to the Sandbur was uneventful, but the tension of having Ripp following her coupled with the idea that someone might try to ambush them from any angle had her gripping the wheel throughout the trip.

She was more than glad when she was finally able to park in front of the guesthouse and equally relieved when Ripp immediately pulled beside her.

Once they were both out of their vehicles, Lucita

waited at the edge of the front yard for him to join her. "Thank you for the escort home," she said, when he finally reached her side. "Do you have time to come in?"

Ripp realized she was probably hungry for any sort of information about the case that he could give her. He had to admit, he was hungry just for her company. It was not an admission that he was proud of. No. He didn't like to think that any woman could make him feel things he'd long put out of his life. But Lucita had touched him someway, somehow. And now he simply wanted to take her into his arms and feel her softness against him.

"After seeing you home safely, I'm officially cut loose."

She smiled at him and he inwardly groaned at the sight of her coral-colored lips curving upward to expose a tiny edge of white teeth. No one had to warn him that to kiss those lips would be his undoing. He already knew that kissing Lucita would seal his fate. All the more reason to keep a safe distance, he reasoned with himself.

Like hell, he thought. Given the chance he'd take every kiss, every caress he could snatch from her before she came to her senses and sent him packing.

"Good," she said. "Then you won't have any reason to hurry away."

Trying not to read too much into that remark, Ripp reached for the bag she was toting and followed her into the bungalow.

They had just passed through a small foyer and were entering the living room, when a door slammed from somewhere in the back of the house and an exchange of voices grew near.

"Sounds like we're not alone," Lucita surmised, then

gestured to her bag that he was carrying. "Just put that down anywhere and have a seat. I'll—"

Before she could finish, Marti and his teenage cousin, Gracia, trotted into the room. Both of them were out of breath as though they'd been hurrying over from the big house.

"Hi, Mom!"

"Hi, Aunt Luci!"

Both kids chimed out the greeting at the same time before they each turned their attention to Ripp. Since Gracia had known him for years, she raced over to him and flung her arms tightly around his waist.

"Hi, Mr. Ripp! It's great to see you! Are you gonna stay for supper? Daddy just sent us over to fetch the two of you."

Touched by Gracia's affectionate greeting, Ripp patted the top of the girl's long brown hair. "I don't know, Gracia. I haven't officially been invited," he said, his gaze sliding over to Lucita.

"You're officially invited," she said with a smile.

Releasing her grip on his waist, Gracia took the bag from his hand and tossed it on a nearby couch. "I'm inviting you, too," the teenager echoed.

Marti, who'd been watching the whole exchange between his cousin and the deputy, hung hesitantly back as though he didn't feel a part of the group.

Understanding social skills were harder for a boy, especially one of Marti's age. Ripp stepped forward and extended his hand to Lucita's son. "Hello, Marti. Nice to see you again."

Marti's handshake was firm, but his words were mumbled with less enthusiasm. "Yeah. Guess you're here to guard my mom."

Earlier in the week Lucita had decided to be as truthful as she could with her son. She'd explained that some unknown person was making threatening demands on the family for money. That much was true and she'd seen no need to bring up the subject of his estranged father. But it was plain to see that the whole situation had affected him.

"Marti!" Lucita quickly scolded. "Ripp isn't guarding me. He's here to make sure everything is okay with the whole family. And you should thank him for that."

"It's okay, Lucita," Ripp softly tossed at her, then with a brief smile, he said to Marti, "I guess I am guarding your mother a little. We wouldn't want anything to happen to her, now would we?"

Marti must have sensed that Ripp was being honest with him, maybe even more honest than most of his family had been, because his whole face suddenly brightened with a grin.

"Yeah. That's right enough. Thank you, Mr. Ripp," he said politely.

Ripp patted the boy on the shoulder. "You're quite welcome."

Coming up behind him, Gracia looped her arm through Ripp's and tugged him forward. "Come on, Mr. Ripp. Everybody's waiting to eat. Brady killed a wild hog while the crew was out on roundup and Juan barbecued the whole thing. And if you don't like that he threw some chickens on the grill, too."

"I'll eat anything," he said as the two kids urged him forward.

Behind the threesome, Lucita thoughtfully watched her son sidle up to Ripp. Ever since Marti had learned about his father's betrayal, she'd feared that he would view all men with suspicion. And that was the last thing she wanted for her son. He needed a masculine mentor, someone other than a family member, but she wasn't sure Ripp could ever be that person. Even though he was a friend of Matt's and Mingo's, she had to remember that he was really here as a duty, not because she and Marti were special people in his life.

"You three go on," she called as they headed out of the living room. "I'm going to take a minute to change clothes. I'll be right there."

Minutes later, after Lucita had changed into a pair of jean shorts and a red tank top with spaghetti straps, she hurried out to the backyard to find the whole area more like a party than anything else.

Tables and chairs had been set up beneath the shade of the pines and palm trees. Music was playing from someone's radio while the smell of roasting meat drifted on the warm humid air. Beer and soda were iced down in a huge galvanized tub and in one corner of the grassy area, Gracia and Marti were tossing a boccie ball.

Lucita walked over to where Juliet was placing a stack of brightly colored melamine plates at the end of one table.

"What's going on?" Lucita asked her sister-in-law. "This is supposed to be High Noon Wednesday, instead we're celebrating—what, I don't know! I thought everyone would be gathered around the phone or the computer or something!"

Turning, the tall blonde gave Lucita a placating smile. "Try to relax, Luci. The FBI is closely monitoring the bank account. A deputy is working undercover at the bank. If a move of any kind takes place, someone will be watching. Besides, I'm sure you'd be the first to agree that we can't sit around terrorized."

Suddenly shamefaced, Lucita nodded. "You're right. I guess I've just been so keyed up and worried that seeing all of this was a shock to my system."

Juliet glanced across the yard to where her husband sat in a lawn chair holding their ten-month-old son, Jess. Her eyes were soft with love as she spoke. "Matt's been strung tighter than a violin string this past week. He needs this." She looked back to Lucita. "And so do you, Luci."

Releasing a long breath, Lucita did her best to give Juliet a bright smile. Her family had sacrificed so much for her, had lovingly gathered her back into their bosom, once she'd come crawling home with a fatherless son and an empty bank account. She already felt awful for disrupting their lives. The last thing she wanted was to cause more unhappiness.

"You're right. If everything is ready, let's give the call to eat!"

An hour later, everyone was stuffed with Juan's delicious supper. The sun had sunk below the western horizon and a southerly breeze was stirring up the humid air.

Marti and Gracia had talked Matt and Juliet into playing a game of boccie ball, so Lucita had offered to keep watch over little Jess while his parents were occupied. At ten months, the toddler had just discovered the art of walking and would quickly become infuriated if anyone tried to keep him in one spot.

Lucita decided the best way to keep the tot happy was to let him walk around the shaded yard and explore. Across the lawn, she could see her father and Ripp sitting at one end of the porch, seemingly engaged in a casual conversation. Every so often Mingo would let out a chuckle and slap his knee. As for Ripp, he appeared more relaxed than she'd ever seen him since this whole nightmare had started.

Maybe this was the beginning of the end, she thought hopefully. If nothing horrible occurred tonight, then perhaps they could count the whole episode with the extortion note as a cruel hoax just to make their lives miserable.

Jess's whimpers suddenly pulled Lucita's mind back to the chore at hand. She glanced down to see her nephew was trying his best to reach for a bright red hibiscus bloom, but his stubby little fingers were at the most, a half foot away.

"Sorry, Jess. You can't pluck the flower. You'd be eating it in about two seconds."

The baby must have understood she was saying no. He strained harder to reach the flower as his whimpers became all-out cries.

"Okay, little man, come here," she crooned to the baby as she stooped to pick him up. "Let's go find something else to interest you."

To the left of the guesthouse the lawn merged with that of the big house. It was here that Mingo had built a gazebo for his beloved wife, Elizabeth. Down through the years the wood had weathered to dove-gray and the whole roof and one side of the structure were completely covered with a tangle of jasmine and moonflower vines. Inside the quiet hideaway, low benches lined the hexagon-shaped floor.

Lucita placed Jess on his feet and his hands on the top of the bench for balance. Realizing he had a whole new world to explore, the baby bounced on his knees and cooed with pleasure.

"Looks like he's happy now."

Ripp's voice had Lucita suddenly whirling to see the

tall, dark deputy climbing the steps to the gazebo. The sight of him never failed to send pleasure spilling through her and she couldn't stop herself from smiling as he ducked his head and entered the vine-draped opening.

"Well, for the moment." Lucita glanced fondly down at the toddler. "Unfortunately, he's like his father. He wants his way and howls if he doesn't get it."

Ripp chuckled. "Oh, well, I expect most men are that way."

She glanced back up at him and was acutely aware that he was standing only inches from her and that the vine-covered sanctuary secluded them from the curious eyes of her family.

"Uh—I thought you and Daddy were having a visit."

"We were. But I noticed Junior crying and thought you might need a little help." He gestured to the bench where Jess was patting the smooth wood with both hands. "Want to sit?"

Glad to comply with his invitation, Lucita sat down a short space over from Jess while Ripp took a seat next to her. Her senses went on instant alert and she had to remind herself to breathe normally, to behave as though he was a friend instead of a tough lawman with sex appeal shouting from his booted feet to the top of his black Stetson.

"So tell me, Deputy McCleod, are you familiar with handling babies?" she asked impishly.

His eyes were unexpectedly provocative as they roamed her face and their touch warmed Lucita's cheeks with color.

He grinned. "Not really. But I can carry and jostle and usually stop them from crying."

"That's a start," she said. "But at the moment Jess seems to be content. Let's hope it stays that way for a few minutes."

Ripp glanced from her to the baby and back again. "You seem very good with him."

Lucita started to laugh, but the sound that passed her lips was more like a strangled groan. "It's been a long time since Marti was this age, but I guess a mother doesn't forget."

He must have picked up on the wistfulness in her voice because he continued to study her in a way that made Lucita feel as though he was slowly peeling away the layers of her thoughts.

"You—uh—never wanted more children?"

There had been other people who had asked her the very same question, but it had never affected her like this. Long-hidden emotions were suddenly lodged in her throat, making her words a strain to get out.

"I would have liked three or four—even five. But Derek insisted one child was all we needed in our lives. I could never change his mind." Sighing, she looked away from his probing gaze. "The way that things worked out I suppose it's best that I didn't get pregnant again."

Ripp looked over at Jess, who'd now decided to get down on all fours and crawl his way to the other side of the gazebo. The boy was the image of his father and Ripp couldn't help but wonder what it would feel like to see a child stamped with his own features and traits, to know that the child was the result of shared love.

"Sorry I asked, Lucita. I didn't mean to bring up sad memories. It's just that you obviously love children—you chose to be a teacher."

Shrugging, she gave him a wobbly smile. "What about yourself? Would you like to have children someday?"

His gaze pulled away from the baby and back to her.

"Me? Well, I don't know." Searching awkwardly for the words to answer her question, he stretched his long legs out in front of him and rubbed his palms down the thighs of his jeans. "It's not something I think about too much. I guess there have been times I've imagined how it might be to have a son or daughter. But in the end, it's hard for me to envision some little soul calling me daddy. You know what I mean?"

He'd hardly gotten the question out when Jess suddenly made a sharp U-turn and scampered straight toward Ripp. The moment he came into contact with his cowboy boots, the baby sat back on his haunches and reached for the dusty soles. Ripp immediately pulled his feet back and stretched out his hand as an aid for Jess to stand.

As the baby gurgled and patted Ripp's knees, Lucita said gently, "I think you'd make a wonderful father."

With his eyes fixed on Matt's son, Ripp said, "I'm thirty-seven, Lucita. It's getting late for me to be thinking about having a family."

Lucita frowned. He was young, strong and virile, a man in the very prime of life. Yet he talked as though he was in the sunset of his days.

"Don't be ridiculous, Ripp. You have plenty of time left. That is, if you want to make the most of it. Or maybe you don't want to be a—family man."

Swinging his head toward hers, she was surprised to see a look of true loneliness on his face. "Heck, Lucita, I don't even have a woman in my life. And even if I did, living with a deputy isn't easy. Pam couldn't take it. She eventually found someone else."

Lucita pursed her lips to a censuring line. Maybe she didn't know Ripp McCleod inside and out, she silently conceded. But she knew enough about him to see that he was a morally upright person, a man that cared about people. He deserved more than a woman cheating behind his back.

"Then that's her loss."

His eyes widened with surprise, then with a shake of his head, he sighed. "Thanks for that. But I don't think you understand, Lucita. I—being a deputy is—well, we just don't have normal lives. And that's what most women want. Stability. Security."

Yes. That's all she'd ever wanted, Lucita thought. A man who came home to her every night, a love so secure that the vow "till death" stood true.

"All lawmen don't live as bachelors. There are plenty of women out there who could deal with your job," she softly suggested. "You just haven't found the right one yet. That is—if you want to look for her."

There was a long, pregnant pause during which little Jess moved farther into the *V* between Ripp's legs.

But she could see that Ripp's attention wasn't on the movements of the curious baby. His gaze was riveted to Lucita's face and as her eyes locked with his, she felt a jolt all the way down to her toes.

There were questions in his eyes; soft, needy questions that couldn't be answered entirely with words. Her racing heart screeched almost to a halt as his head slowly dipped toward hers.

"I am looking for her, Lucita," he murmured. "I'm looking right now."

Sensing what was coming, she tried to speak his name, warn him in some way that what he was about to do was fruitless, that she wasn't ready to enter into a relationship. But, except for a tiny gasp of much-needed air, nothing would pass her lips.

Numbly, she realized she could duck her head or jump to her feet and run like a scared rabbit. But those fleeting thoughts didn't stand a chance against the delicious anticipation zipping through her veins. And instead of resisting, something deep within had her leaning toward him, tilting her head so that her lips were totally available to his.

When his mouth finally made contact with hers Lucita was certain she'd jumped into a whirlwind. All she could hear was the roar of her pounding heart. All she could feel was the hard plunder of his lips as they coaxed and tasted and teased until she finally groaned with surrender and wrapped her arms around his neck.

Somewhere in the back of her mind she could hear her family tossing comments back and forth across the lawn, could sense little Jess moving about their tangled knees, but everything else was quickly fading as she began to sink and drown in a pool of desire.

Chapter Seven

It was Jess's fussy whimpers that finally entered Lucita's awareness and reminded her that the kiss had gone on far too long. In fact, it could no longer be called simply a kiss. It was an all-out heated embrace and her face felt scorched as she disengaged her fingers from the back of his neck and eased her mouth away.

"I—uh—" She gulped for air and looked down at Jess, who was tugging at the hem of her shorts and beginning to cry with frustration. Obviously the child was tired of being ignored. "I think Jess needs to find his parents."

Quickly, before Ripp could make any sort of reply, she rose to her feet. But as she bent to lift the toddler into her arms, he brushed her to one side.

"Let me," he said huskily. "He's a hefty little guy."

Ripp picked up the boy and adjusted the baby's weight in the crook of one arm. Immediately Jess was pacified and his tiny hand went straight to the shiny badge pinned to the left pocket on Ripp's shirt.

While the baby amused himself, Ripp turned his gaze to Lucita. Even in the gloaming of the evening he could see she'd been shaken by what had just taken place. Her hands were trembling as she attempted to smooth her tangled hair and the muscles in her throat worked as she swallowed not once, but twice.

"Lucita," he said softly. "I hope you're not upset with me."

That swung her gaze up to his and he watched a somewhat comical frown pucker her forehead. "Upset? Ripp, I—" She stopped, drew in a long breath, then released a strangled laugh. "I wasn't exactly trying to get away, now was I?"

The fact that she wasn't trying to be coy or evasive encouraged Ripp and assured him that he'd not mistaken the taste of hunger and longing on her lips. Yet knowing that wasn't enough to ease the awkwardness of the moment. He felt like a very young man, bowled over by a sudden rush of tender emotions and not doing very well at hiding them.

"Lucita," he said her name again, this time even softer. "I want you to know that I…didn't plan for that to happen. But I—I couldn't stop myself from showing you how I feel."

Her features took on a strained look as she continued to gaze up at him. "And how do you feel, Ripp?"

How did he feel? In truth, he could hardly contain himself. He wanted to jump up and down and shout with sheer joy. He wanted to pull her back into his arms and kiss her until they were both drunk, to hold her against him and feel the warmth of her body giving life to his.

But Jess was wedged between them and with the rest of her family only a few feet away, he could hardly do any of those things.

With a short shake of his head, he said, "I don't know—I just know that I care about you, Lucita. Maybe more than I should."

Pressing her lips together, she glanced away from him and wiped a shaky hand over her face. "I care about you, too, Ripp, but I—"

Sensing she was about to go into a laundry list of why they shouldn't get involved with each other, he reached out and closed a hand over her shoulder.

"Let's not go into buts, Lucita," he said gently. "It's clear that you have a lot on your mind now. And so do I. My main concern is you. And keeping you and your family safe."

His kiss hadn't felt like that of a guardian, Lucita thought unsteadily. Oh God, her knees were still threatening to buckle and her lips burned with the imprint of his. She'd been kissed many times before in her life, but not one of them had tilted her world as this one had.

It's pure chemistry, Lucita. The man is good-looking and drenched with sexuality. It's natural that he stirred you up.

If it hadn't been for the soft, gooey feeling in her heart, the arguments in her head could have won the reasoning war. But at the moment that tender spot in her chest was dictating all her thoughts.

"And that's why you're here." She murmured the reminder more to herself than to him, but he obviously heard it. The hand that was curved possessively around her shoulder now slipped upward until his fingertips were brushing temptingly against her cheek.

"You think this is part of my normal duties as a county deputy?"

How could she think? How could she answer anything when his touch was warming spots inside her that she'd believed had long turned to ice?

"No."

Her one word was enough to curve his lips with a faint smile.

"Good."

She smiled back at him and as their gazes merged and lingered, she felt her heart leap, her breath catch in her throat. If he kissed her again, she'd be totally lost.

But apparently kissing her had left his mind. Instead, he moved his hand to the middle of her back and urged her toward the opening of the gazebo.

"We'd better get back to the rest of your family," he told her. "Or they're going to come looking for us."

The next day passed in an anticlimactic way for everyone on the Sandbur, especially Lucita. Thankfully, nothing seemed to have happened in lieu of their decision to keep the million dollars out of the mystery bank account. Undercover officers had kept a continual watch in and out of the bank. Hired guards had been posted at the lone front entrance to the Sandbur and Frank, the wrangler, once again took up his vigilant task of driving behind Lucita back and forth to work. Nothing strange or even remotely suspicious had happened and for the first time since her car accident, Lucita began to relax.

Thursday passed and then Friday. By the time Saturday rolled around even Matt had begun to smile and when he and Juliet asked if Marti could attend the rodeo at Victoria with them and Gracia, she didn't hesitate to give her son permission to go.

Even though her son hadn't exhibited any signs of undue stress, she knew a night of relaxation with his cousin would be good for him. And seeing all the horses and excitement at the rodeo would be a perfect tonic.

Later that evening, Marti stood in the doorway of her makeshift office, thoughtfully regarding his mother while Lucita worked on lesson plans.

"Are you sure you don't want to go, Mom? Uncle Matt says there'll be some dandy bull riders there. And there's supposed to be some sort of trick act where a dog rides on the back of a horse." His mouth twisted with disbelief and he shook his head. "I don't believe it. Ain't no horse in Texas gonna let a dog on its back, that's for sure."

"There *isn't* a horse," Lucita automatically corrected his grammar. "And Texas is a mighty big state. There might be one horse who likes to carry a dog on its back."

"Shoot, I won't believe that until I see it."

Smiling, Lucita looked up to see that Marti had changed into clean jeans and shirt and had pulled on his best cowboy boots, but had chosen to wear the most crumpled straw hat he owned.

"Marti! Your grandfather just bought you a new hat a few weeks ago. Why aren't you wearing it?"

He tilted his head from side to side as he considered her question. "Well, Gracia says she's wearing her old hat 'cause she don't want to look like some greenhorn dude. Especially if any boys look at her." He stopped long enough to roll his eyes. "She wants to be cool."

"What about you?"

He hung his thumbs in the belt loops on the front of

his jeans and spread his legs in a stance that resembled an Old West gunfighter. "Well, I don't want to look like a tenderfoot, either."

The smile on Lucita's face deepened to a teasing grin. "Especially if some girls just happened to take a look at you?"

"Awww, Mom!" he squealed with indignation. "You know I'm not old enough to have a girlfriend! And even if I was, I don't want one! Girls are silly and scared of their own shadows. I doubt I'll ever like one."

Totally amused by her son's attitude, she couldn't let it drop. "You like me, don't you?"

To her surprise he scurried into the room and wrapped his arms around her neck in a tight hug. "You're different, Mom. I love you."

For the past year Marti had considered himself too grown-up to show displays of affection toward his mother. She couldn't figure what had gotten into him this evening, but his sweet response choked her with emotions.

Swallowing, she patted his back. "I love you, too, honey."

Just as quickly as the hug had started, Marti jumped from his mother and with an impish grin raced toward the door. "I'd better get over to the big house before Uncle Matt leaves without me!"

As his boots echoed through the hallway, Lucita called out after him, "Behave, Marti. And don't wander away from your aunt and uncle."

"I won't, Mom."

"Have a good time."

"I will!"

After that she could hear the back door open and

close with a rapid bang. With a wistful sigh, she immediately reached for the phone and dialed her brother's number.

Thankfully, Matt answered on the second ring.

"Marti is on his way over," she said to him. "Please, Matt, keep an eye on him. If something happened I—"

"Stop," he firmly interrupted. "Just stop all this worrying, Luci. Between me and Juliet and Gracia we'll keep a close eye on him. Besides, I don't think Derek has the nerve to try anything. I think he sees that the law is watching him like a hound after a squirrel."

Lucita rolled her eyes. She still wasn't convinced that Derek had any part of her car accident or the threatening note, but now wasn't the time to argue with her brother. "Okay. I won't worry. We have to go on living our lives, don't we?"

"There's never been a Saddler or Sanchez to run and hide from trouble. We're not about to start now."

He was right. She wasn't a coward. And she couldn't make Marti live in seclusion. "You're right. And thanks, Matt, for inviting him. He needs this sort of normal fun."

"Yeah. And so do you. Are you sure you don't want to come along, too? There's still time for you to get changed or whatever you need to do to get ready."

"Thanks, but I've got plenty here to keep me busy. And besides, it will make Marti feel grown-up to be on an outing without his mother along."

"Marti's here," Matt announced. "I'll talk to you later. And it will probably be late when we get home so I'll keep Marti for the night. He likes to sleep in the nursery with Jess. I think he's trying to tell us he'd like a sibling, Luci."

Trying to take his comment as a joke, she laughed lightly. "Well, that would be a miracle, now wouldn't it?"

"Not really," he said, then before she could make any sort of reply, he added, "Good night, Luci."

Thirty minutes later, Lucita had finished her lesson plans and was trying to get interested in a comedy on the television. But her wandering mind couldn't focus on the plot.

She hadn't seen Ripp since Wednesday evening when they'd shared that torrid embrace, but she had spoken to him yesterday afternoon.

The call had been quick and professional; a few words to assure her that Sheriff Travers was continuing to keep her case on the front burner. She'd been grateful for the update, but she'd been even happier to hear his voice, which had been soft and husky, hinting but not confessing outright that his thoughts had been on her, too.

Letting Ripp consume her mind was ridiculous, she told herself as she reached for the remote control and punched the off button. But his company made her happy. Very happy.

On that light note, she walked over to the telephone and picked up the little book where she'd stored his cell phone number.

Ripp was a few minutes away from the Dry Gulch Saloon on the outskirts of Goliad when his cell phone shrilled above the country music playing on the radio.

Expecting that his time off and the beer he'd been planning on having would have to be put on hold, he pulled the instrument from his pocket and quickly flipped it open.

Not bothering to look at the ID, he reached to turn down the radio at the same time as he said, "McCleod here."

"Ripp. This is Lucita. Have I caught you at a bad time?"

Totally surprised by the sound of Lucita's voice, he whipped the truck onto the shoulder of the highway. "Lucita. Is anything wrong?"

"No."

She let out a short laugh that sounded oddly nervous, but before he could ask her what the call was about, she spoke again. "The house is empty. Marti went to a rodeo with Matt and his family. Now I'm wandering through the rooms wondering what I'm going to do for the rest of the evening. I thought I'd call and see if—if you're not busy maybe you'd like to come over. If you haven't eaten anything we could grill something. I have wieners and ground chuck in the fridge. I might even be able to scrounge up a beer or two."

Ripp was fairly stunned by her invitation. Even though she had given him that mind-blowing kiss in the gazebo, he'd left the Sandbur Wednesday night certain that she would never allow anything personal to grow between them. Had he misread her subtle signals, or did she simply want to talk to him about the department's work on the extortion note?

Hell, it didn't matter why she was inviting him. He was glad. Damn glad.

"I'll be there in fifteen minutes," he said, then ended the call and made a quick U-turn in the middle of the highway.

Thirty minutes later, he was sitting with Lucita beneath the shade of a Mexican palm, drinking a beer and waiting for the charcoal to burn to a nice bed of coals.

Twilight had fallen and Lucita had lit several bamboo torches to ward away the mosquitoes flying around the yard. As Ripp watched the flickering fingers of light dance upon her lovely face, he wondered if he should pinch himself to make sure he was awake.

Maybe he was really at the Dry Gulch and had fallen asleep at the bar, because this was more like a pleasant dream than Ripp's day-to-day reality.

"I've got to admit your call really surprised me, Lucita. But I'm very glad you made it."

She glanced at him and then quickly turned her gaze away as though she was still a bit embarrassed by the whole thing. Sighing, she said, "I hope you don't think…well, I'm not in the habit of calling a man…not for any reason. And I wouldn't have called you tonight but—" She broke off awkwardly as she turned her gaze back to him. "I like being with you, Ripp. And I think you like being with me. I hope you didn't come tonight just out of a sense of duty…or because my brother is one of your best friends."

Even before she finished speaking, Ripp was out of his chair and squatting next to hers. Taking her hand in his, he squeezed it gently. "Lucita, I'm here because of you. Only you. I think…the other night when we kissed I thought…I was trying to tell you then how I felt about you."

She released a shaky breath and her fingers curled tightly around his. "I've tried not to think too much about that kiss, Ripp."

Tonight she was wearing a sundress printed in big blue-and-white flowers. Skinny straps held up the top while the neck dipped low enough to expose a smooth slope of cleavage. His eyes could hardly stay off her honey-brown skin and now he had to fight to keep his hands from touching her.

"Why?"

Bending her head, she murmured, "Because it makes me think about things that—well, that I shouldn't be thinking about."

"Like making love?" he asked huskily. Just saying the words out loud to her was enough to send a rush of desire straight to his loins. What would it do to him if he actually went to bed with her, he wondered wildly.

"Yes," she said in a voice so low he could hardly hear it.

Drawing in a deep breath, he allowed his hand to glide up her arm until he reached a strand of her light brown hair. As he twisted the silky lock around his finger, he moved his face closer to hers.

The scent of jasmine and some other sweet-smelling flower emanated from her skin and swirled around his already-scattered senses. In response, his eyelids drifted downward, but he stopped them short of closing. There was too much beauty in front of him and he didn't want to miss seeing any of it.

"Lucita, this thing between us—it scares me, too. I never expected some woman to come along and shake me up the way you have."

Lifting her head, she gazed at him in a troubled, almost resigned way. "I never thought I'd want another man. Ever."

Her voice was strained and edged with longing. The sound of it pushed Ripp's heart into quick, hard thuds.

"Do you want me, Lucita?"

Closing her eyes, she leaned her face toward his. "More than I can tell you."

He needed to breathe, to suck in enough oxygen to clear his head. But as his lips met hers, he realized he didn't care if he was thinking or not. Kissing her, touching her, was all that mattered.

Above the roar of hot blood rushing through his ears, he could hear her groan of surrender. A burst of incredible triumph shot through him as her arms wrapped around his neck and her mouth opened beneath his.

He kissed her hungrily, thoroughly, until the burning in his legs forced him to break contact with her and rise from his squatting position.

With her head tilted at a provocative angle, she looked up at him questioningly and he offered his hand to her.

Wordlessly she allowed him to draw her out of the wicker chair and into his arms. After another slow kiss that had his insides burning, she pulled away.

"Let's go to the porch," she whispered.

If necessary, Ripp would have followed her through a hoop of fire. And maybe he was doing just that, he thought. He certainly felt as though every inch of him was smoldering as she led him into the dark shadows beneath the overhang of the porch.

Moments later they reached a cushioned lounge positioned at the far end of the porch and she quickly tugged him down beside her.

Stirred even more by her boldness, Ripp wrapped her close to him and his fingers began a slow dance over the skin of her shoulders.

"Are you sure no one will be coming around?" He mouthed the question against her cheek.

"Dad is over at Geraldine's and everyone else is gone," she said in a husky rush. "There's no one to interrupt us."

The idea was enough to cause his hand to tremble as he pushed a wave of tumbled hair off her forehead. "Lucita, I—" He swallowed as he tried to gather himself together enough to speak all the things that were clamoring to get out of his heart. "I never dreamed I would ever be here with you like this. I never thought that you…well, that you could ever want someone like me."

Even though it was too dark to clearly see the expression on her face, he could hear a puzzled note in her words. "What do you mean? Why wouldn't I want someone like you?" Then her soft hands clasped his cheeks, touching him as though he were precious.

Slowly his hands met at the small of her back, then glided upward until his fingers were touching the exposed skin along her shoulder blades. She was as soft as butter on a hot afternoon.

"Why?" he repeated wryly. "Lucita, you belong to a rich, notable family. That pretty much says it all."

With a short shake of her head, she said, "Having money in the bank or nice clothes doesn't make me any different from other women. I have the same needs and wants, Ripp."

He rubbed his cheek against hers. "You can have the best of everything, Lucita."

Her hands tightened along his back as a sigh slipped past her lips and skittered across his ear. "Have you ever stopped to think that I might have the best right here next to me?"

A rough chuckle rumbled in his throat. "I didn't know you were such a flatterer, Lucita. And you don't have to be, you know," he murmured. "You and me like this is enough."

"Ripp, you—"

He interrupted with a hungry growl. "We've got better things to do than talk, Lucita."

To prove it, he eased them both down on the cushioned lounge and began to kiss her. This time he didn't hold back in showing her exactly how much he wanted her.

His fingers plowed into her hair and cradled the back of her head while his tongue plunged into her welcoming mouth. The helpless moan that sounded in her throat fueled his need to get even closer.

Without breaking the kiss, his hands spread against her back and urged her to lie on her side facing him. Once the front of her body was pressing against his, he lost all sense of their surroundings and the long, long minutes ticking by.

The only thing Ripp knew was that her soft mouth was nibbling at his; her hands were exploring his arms, chest and face. Along the length of him, he could feel her breasts pressing into his arm and a part of his chest, her hips pushing against the aching bulge behind the fly of his jeans. Heat spiraled through him and sent gray smoke curling around his senses, obscuring everything but the urgent need to make love to her.

At some point the contact of their lips was broken and he used the moment to allow his mouth to explore the tender curve of her throat, the velvety smooth skin sloping to her breast.

His fingers were pulling the strap of her sundress down on her arm, his mouth seeking the ripe center of one breast, when the faint sound of his cell phone punctured the quietness of the night.

For long moments, Ripp ignored the ring, his mind and his body refusing to relinquish the paradise of her embrace. But as the caller persisted, he could sense Lucita stilling beneath him. Finally she asked in a thick voice, "Should you answer that?"

Wiping a hand over his face, he eased away from her and pulled the phone from his jean pocket.

"I'm off duty right now. But that doesn't mean a hill of beans if something has happened and the sheriff needs me," he said to her as he quickly flipped open the cell phone and answered, "McCleod here."

"Ripp, where are you?"

Instantly identifying Matt's voice, Ripp rose to his feet as though his friend could see just how close he was to his sister.

"I'm—uh—actually, I'm here at Lucita's house. Is something wrong?"

"Hell yeah, something's wrong!" he practically shouted back. "Marti is missing! We think someone took him! He and Gracia went to the concession stand for something to eat. Marti waited in line while Gracia went to the restroom. When she got back, he wasn't anywhere to be found."

Icy fear plummeted through Ripp as he glanced at Lucita. If anything happened to Marti, her life would be totally devastated.

"Where are you now?"

"Still at the rodeo—the old arena—at the river park."

"Have you called the police? Has Sheriff Travers been notified?"

"I called the police, they're all over the rodeo grounds and the rest of the park. They're not letting anyone enter or leave. But this is Victoria County, Ripp. Travers—"

"Knows the case," Ripp quickly interrupted. "I— we'll be there shortly, Matt."

He snapped the phone shut, then drawing in a bracing breath looked over at Lucita who, at some point during the call, had risen from the lounge and was now standing at his side.

"It's Marti, isn't it?"

Even in the shadows, her oval face was deathly pale and utterly still except for her trembling lips. He desperately wanted to take her into his arms and reassure her, but there wasn't time for anything except the truth.

"Yes. They can't find him and Matt thinks someone has taken him."

"Oh God," she whispered starkly. Then grabbing his arm, she shook it almost violently. "Ripp, that can't be! Tell me you're lying!"

Wrapping his arm around her shoulders, he urged her toward the back entrance of the house. "I wish I were, Lucita. Right now, you need to gather your purse or whatever you need with you. I told Matt we were on our way."

The urgency in his voice seemed to get through to her, but as they reached the door, she paused and with a muffled cry, buried her face in his chest and began to sob.

"Ripp! You've got to get my son back," she cried. "Promise me!"

Choking down the emotions in his throat, he soothed a hand over the top of her head. "I promise to get your son back, Lucita. Or die trying."

Chapter Eight

The thirty-minute drive into Victoria passed in a nightmarish daze for Lucita. It only got worse when they entered the southeastern side of the city and began to encounter roadblocks and jammed lines of traffic.

Once Ripp flashed his badge, a path was made for them to pass, but the going was slow. As the truck inched its way through the stalled traffic, Lucita had to fight to keep from bursting into sobs and screaming at the top of her lungs.

"I…can't think that someone—someone evil has my boy," Lucita choked out for the third time since they'd entered the city. "I'm trying not to let myself imagine what he might be going through right now. But I—I can't stop myself, Ripp! Oh, God," she prayed aloud, "Please let him be found safe and sound."

Reaching over, Ripp gripped her hand. "Try not to

think the worst, Lucita. I know that's a damn lame thing to say, but you can't let your imagination take over."

Wiping at her tears, she swallowed and nodded. "You're right. Yes, you're right. I'll try."

The sight of her so crushed and distraught was like a sledgehammer hitting him right in the heart. He didn't want her to hurt for one second, for any reason. But he feared she was going to have to endure even more pain before Marti was found.

When they finally reached the rodeo grounds they discovered police, deputies, sheriffs from two counties and even a pair of Texas Rangers, who happened to be in the area, had swarmed all over the river park and the arena.

Barriers were erected on side streets and lights were whirling and flashing over the crowds of people spread over the immediate vicinity. Sirens blew out warnings while shouts mingled with loud conversation and even the sound of laughter.

Without Ripp by her side, she would have never been allowed into the chaotic mess of people and lawmen doing their best to interrogate and prevent anyone from leaving the area. But eventually, after a bit of explanation and Ripp's identification, they were allowed to walk to the rodeo arena to find Lucita's family.

Matt was waiting near the entrance with Juliet and Gracia standing closely behind him. Juliet looked dazed with fear, while Matt looked outright furious. But it was Gracia that caught Lucita's attention. She was crying openly and glancing around the restless crowd as though she was hoping beyond hope that her little cousin would reappear.

"Any news?" Ripp asked Matt as the other man enfolded Lucita in a brief embrace.

"We've not heard anything, other than being told that no one is allowed in or out of the park. But I guess you could see all the roadblocks."

Grim faced, Ripp nodded. "As we made our way in here, I talked to a couple of Victoria County deputies. They didn't have anything new."

Standing in the curve of Matt's arm, Lucita tried not to let her panic show. "Do any of you have an idea how long Marti has been missing?"

Juliet glanced at her watch. "The moment Gracia came running back to us was about nine-thirty. That's a little more than an hour ago."

Trying to sniffle back her tears, Gracia remorsefully shook her head. "It's all my fault, Aunt Lucita. I shouldn't have gone to the restroom and left him standing there alone. If I'd stayed there he wouldn't be—he might not be—no one could have taken him!" she finally finished with a broken sob.

Stepping away from her brother, Lucita wrapped her arms around her niece. Gracia was obviously torturing herself with unwarranted guilt, but the teenager couldn't be feeling nearly as guilty as Lucita was at that moment. While someone had been kidnapping her child, she'd been in Ripp's arms, practically begging him to make love to her.

The whole idea was obscene. If anything happened to her son, she'd never forgive herself.

"Gracia, don't be silly. If anyone is guilty around here, it's me. I should have never allowed Marti to come here tonight. Not with the threat that's been hanging over our head."

Matt frowned at his sister and his daughter. "Now

isn't the time for self-recriminations from you two or any of us," he said sharply. "It's pointless. We've got to focus on finding Marti." He looked at Ripp. "What happens now? We can't get a damn bit of information from anyone around here!"

Ripp had to force himself to concentrate on his friend's question. "Everyone is busy trying to do their part, Matt. But I can tell you that a missing child alert has already been sent out over the airwaves. And obviously the immediate area is being searched. If Marti isn't found here, I imagine the Rangers will widen the investigation until he's found. Meanwhile, we wait and see if anyone comes forward with demands."

Matt's expression was murderous. "For money. A child for money! If that bastard Derek has done this, I'll kill him myself!"

At that moment Lucita's legs gave way. She would have fallen to the ground if Ripp's quick reflexes hadn't grabbed her and steadied her in the circle of his arm.

Looking up at him, she pleaded tearfully, "Take me out of this crowd, Ripp."

Hours later, Lucita was sitting in the back of a patrol car as night turned into morning. The huge crowd that had attended the rodeo had eventually dwindled to a few stragglers. Some of those had volunteered to stay behind and search the banks of the Guadalupe, the deep river that curved through the city park.

Lucita wouldn't allow herself to think about Marti possibly being in the river. The idea was too horrendous for her to comprehend. Besides, logic told her that if the kidnapper's intention was to use Marti as leverage for money, then the child would be far more useful alive than dead. It was a thought she mentally repeated to herself over and over.

By midmorning Lucita was numb with exhaustion and the shock that her child was well and truly gone from her grasp. Ripp, who'd quickly slipped into the role of deputy once he'd settled her inside the patrol car, had been tied up with duties, but eventually found time to return to the car where she'd been waiting.

Bending his head, he peered into the open window. "Where's Matt?"

"He was needed at the ranch—some emergency with a cattle buyer," Lucita explained. "He didn't want to go, but I made him."

Ripp nodded in approval. "It's time I took you home, too. There's nothing more that you can do here, Lucita. And from what I can gather from the Rangers, they want to set up a listening device on your home telephone. You'll be more help there."

He opened the door of the squad car and extended a helping hand down to her. For one brief moment as Lucita curled her fingers around his, she recalled another time not so long ago that he'd helped her out of a wreck. But this time the crisis wasn't a car crash; it was the life of her son.

"I'm afraid to leave, Ripp. I keep thinking he'll come walking up and that this whole thing will be just a horrible joke."

Not caring that there were others around to see, Ripp gathered her against his chest and stroked her hair. "I'm afraid this isn't a joke, Lucita. But everything is going to be all right. I promise."

Tilting her head back, she searched his face. "You can't make a promise like that, Ripp. You don't know what's going to happen."

Stroking his fingers against her temple, he said, "No. Maybe not. But I have faith. And you should, too."

Somehow Lucita made it back to the Sandbur without falling asleep, but later when Ripp insisted she lie down on the couch while he made coffee, she slipped off into a fitful doze and didn't rouse until she heard voices coming from the foyer.

After that, the house immediately filled up with lawmen, who quickly took control of her home and every communication device that she owned. Two Texas Rangers interrogated her, even though she'd already spent hours answering questions while she'd waited in the patrol car back in Victoria.

Thankfully Ripp stayed at her side throughout the questioning and his reassuring presence lent her the strength to give them the complete answers they needed. But the experience left Lucita feeling like a bug under a microscope and even more stupid for allowing Marti out of her sight in the first place.

By midafternoon, the whole ranch was being searched and employees questioned. Lucita had been ordered to stay put, and though she wanted to race out and start combing every mile between the Sandbur and Victoria, she realized the best way to find Marti was to get some sort of contact from the kidnapper.

It came that night. Lucita was sitting in Marti's room, her troubled gaze on her son's favorite books and videos, his baseball and glove, and the handmade spurs that his grandfather had given him on his last birthday. Would he ever be home to enjoy riding over the Sandbur range with Gracia again? Or was yesterday the last time she would ever see her son?

No, she scolded herself. She couldn't allow her

thoughts to go in that ghastly direction. She had to keep hoping. Keep praying that she would soon have her son back in her arms.

A brief knock on the door had her turning to see Ripp entering the small bedroom. She stared at him numbly.

"Did you hear the telephone ringing?" he asked.

She had. But there had been numerous calls throughout the afternoon and none of them had been more than friends and acquaintances wanting to express their concern or offer their help. Some calls had even been marketers trying to sell their wares and after a while Lucita had forced herself to ignore the phone. Otherwise, she was going to fall apart each time it rang.

"I did. Is someone wanting to speak to me?" At the moment she didn't think she could summon enough energy to hold a conversation with anyone.

"No."

He stepped forward and she thought she recognized a spark of hope on his face. Instantly, she crossed the room to him.

"What is it?" she asked urgently.

"Matt just talked to the kidnapper."

His blunt words were so unexpected and frightening that her legs threatened to buckle and she used both fists to snatch a hold on the front of his shirt.

"Are you—how can you be sure? The caller could be playing a cruel hoax."

"Matt spoke to Marti. Only for a brief moment. Just long enough to hear his voice, but it was enough to tell us that he's alive and well."

"Oh God! Oh, thank God for that much!"

The deluge of relief rushing through her was so great

that her body began to melt and slide down the front of him. Quick to react, Ripp gathered her up in his arms and carried her over to the bed.

After he'd set her on the edge of the mattress, he wiped a hand over her pale face. It was clammy and he frowned as he realized she'd come close to fainting.

"Lucita, you need a doctor! I'm having Matt call your cousin or her husband."

Bending her head, she gulped in several long breaths. "No, I—Nicci's pregnant. Ridge needs to keep her home and out of this chaos."

Seeming to collect herself, she reached for him and Ripp sat next to her. Her fingers wrapped around his forearm and clung as though he was the only thing keeping her afloat. The idea filled his heart with bittersweet emotion. From the moment he'd met this woman he'd wanted her to need him. And now that she did, he realized he'd cut off the very arm she was holding to get her son back and make her happy again.

With a shake of her head, she met his gaze. "I'm all right now. Just tell me. Everything. What does this person want? Could Matt tell who the caller was?"

He grimaced. "The voice was disguised. Something had apparently been wrapped around the receiver of the phone to muffle the voice. Whoever the caller, he or she is demanding that two million dollars be dropped at a certain location tomorrow night at eight o'clock. Once this person picks up the money, he or she will leave instructions as to where to find Marti."

She stared at him and he could see all sorts of questions and scenarios clicking through her head.

"Two million! That's different from the extortion note." A deep furrow appeared between her brows.

"Maybe this is someone entirely different, Ripp. Someone else wanting money from the family!"

Ripp shook his head. "No, it's the same person. The caller said he upped the amount because you didn't comply with his first request."

"Bastard!" Lucita muttered through clenched teeth. "If this is Derek and we find him, I'm going to get one of Daddy's rifles and blow a hole right through him! He'll wish to hell he'd never crossed me!"

The fire and vengeance burning in her eyes told him that Lucita wasn't as meek and delicate as she appeared on the outside, but that hardly surprised him. The Sandbur families had a reputation for being tough. Lucita was born from ancestors who'd fought Comancheros, Santa Anna's Mexican Army, and even cattle rustlers to settle this tough land. She had a fighting spirit bred in her genes and now that her son was in danger, it was coming to the surface.

"I feel the same way, Lucita. But forget that kind of talk. Derek, or whoever—once the person is caught he'll be punished for this in a court of law, I promise."

Her lips pressed together and then tears spilled onto her pale cheeks. "God, you must think I'm awful, Ripp. I'm so sorry you're seeing me like this—I'm not a murderer. I'm just furious and frightened. And I can't bear to think of what might happen to Marti. What am I supposed to do?"

Stroking a soothing hand down the side of her hair, he said, "I could never think you're awful. You're a strong and wonderful woman. And right now Matt, Lex and your father are discussing plans with Sheriff Travers and the Rangers. Are you up to joining them?"

Nodding, she started to rise, then, still gripping his arm, she paused long enough to press a kiss to his cheek.

"You won't leave me, will you?"

Her whispered question puckered his brow. "Why would I do something like that?"

Shrugging, she glanced away from him. "I understand it's your job to help find Marti. But it isn't your duty to be here with me—like this. I'm afraid that—this is all so ugly, Ripp. And I—"

Taking her by the shoulder, he turned her upper body so that she was facing him. "We're going to get through this, Lucita. Together. And when it's over you and I are—"

"I can't think about that—us, now, Ripp," she interrupted. Her eyes were shadowed and pleading. "You understand, don't you?"

Of course he understood. Still, it would have been nice to hear that no matter what happened in the next few days, she considered him a part of her future. Smiling wanly, he said, "Completely. Now we'd better go see what's being planned."

Ripp helped her up and in a matter of moments they entered the living room. At the moment the space looked more like the innards of a police precinct than someone's home. A long, portable table had been set up and was now covered with laptop computers, phones and other technical devices that Lucita didn't recognize.

At the moment, her brother, father and cousin Lex were in deep discussion with Sheriff Travers and the two Rangers who'd been on the case since Marti had gone missing last night.

"I don't think we have a choice here," Lex was saying. "The money is nothing compared to getting Marti back. I'll call our banks and see what I can do about gathering the cash."

Mingo nodded in agreement. "I have the money. And I want my grandchild back. No matter what the cost."

Sheriff Travers, a tall, dark-haired man with a rough-hewn face, spoke up. "Mingo, this person was smart enough to get phony ID, set up an untraceable bank account and track Marti to the rodeo. We've got to assume he's smart enough to know how many large bills it would require to make two million dollars. I'm thinking we could use counterfeit bills wrapped beneath a few real ones. That way if something goes wrong all wouldn't be lost."

Matt instantly barked a protest. "Why take that chance? If this maniac takes the time to count the money and realizes we've duped him, who's to say he might not kill Marti in retaliation?"

"Who's to say he might not kill the boy anyway?" Dale, the older of the Rangers, put in. "In cases like this, there are always risks we, as law officials, have to take. We'll fit the money, real and counterfeit, into two bags and pray the bastard doesn't stop to count it. "

Feeling as though they were discussing some crazy movie plot rather than the recovery of her son, Lucita joined the group of men.

To Matt and Lex, she said firmly, "We're going to do exactly what these lawmen tell us." She turned to Sheriff Travers and the Rangers. "Where do I fit in?"

Jeff, the younger Ranger, politely inclined his head toward Lucita. "Ma'am, you'll be dropping off the money."

"What?"

The one word from Ripp exploded in the room. He didn't care if it looked unprofessional; he curled his arm protectively around Lucita's shoulders.

"It's one of the kidnapper's demands, Ripp," Travers answered. "We might get by with fooling them on the amount of money, but apparently this person *knows* Lucita and can recognize her. We don't want to get that close and then blow this whole thing."

"I still say no!" Ripp argued. "She's not trained and anything could happen!"

"We don't intend to let Ms. Sanchez make this drop alone," the elder Ranger spoke up. "Even though the kidnapper expects her to be alone, someone will have to be hidden in the vehicle."

"That someone will be me," Ripp said before anyone else had a chance to speak.

Lucita could feel Ripp's hand tightening on her shoulder while she watched Matt and Lex exchange knowing glances. What were her brother and cousin thinking? That Ripp's protective attitude toward her meant more than the concern of a dedicated lawman?

Maybe it did, Lucita thought, and maybe at this moment she needed to believe that Ripp actually cared for her as a man cares for a woman; that he would stand at her side, supporting her as a husband would.

But he wasn't her husband, she sadly reminded herself. And he'd not given her any hint that he ever wanted to be. This whole mess had reminded her that one mistake in matrimony was all she ever intended to make.

The following day passed in an anxious blur for Lucita. She tried to eat and rest. She tried to put up a brave and positive front in front of her family. But underneath it all, she was shaking with fear, her mind whirling with all the things that could go right and wrong with the evening ahead.

As for Ripp, she'd not seen him since he'd left the house last night and today as she'd waited for time to pass, she'd caught herself watching out the window for him to appear and wondering how he'd become so essential to her.

"Sit down, Luci. Relax. It will be a while yet before things go into motion. You need to be rested and mentally alert before you and Ripp head out tonight."

This advice was from her cousin, Nicci. In spite of her fears and anxiety, it made Lucita's heart glad to see her. The woman was seven months pregnant and wildly in love with her husband. God only knew the suffering Nicci had gone through during those years she'd been married to Bill. He'd been a cheater and a user, and Lucita didn't know how her cousin had ever found the courage to give her heart to another man. But maybe Nicci had known in her heart that Ridge was the right man. Still, once upon a time Lucita had believed Derek was the right man for her. Instead he'd stolen her money, abandoned her and their son, and could possibly be behind the nightmare going on now.

Rubbing her sweaty hands down the sides of her jeans, Lucita glanced over at Nicci, who was sitting in an armchair with her feet propped on a matching footstool. The two of them were in Lucita's bedroom, trying to find a spot of privacy amidst the troop of law officials that continued to swoop around in the house.

"I know you're right, Nicci. But I can't relax. I'm scared to death."

The other woman sighed. "Yes, I suppose your blood would have to be made of ice water to make yourself relax at a time like this. To be honest, Luci, I'm scared to death, too. But I have faith in the officers working this case."

Lucita glanced at Nicci as she forced herself to sit on the edge of the mattress. "I'm worried about Daddy. Have you taken a look at him? I don't think he's slept a wink since this whole thing started."

Nicci let out a short laugh. "Mingo is a tough man. He doesn't want to be coddled, especially by a doctor."

A grimace tightened Lucita's already strained features. "I don't care what he wants. It hasn't been that long since he recovered from his brain surgery. If all this stress does something to him—" She blew out a heavy breath. "I—can't imagine losing him, too."

Nicci rose from the chair and took a seat next to Lucita, putting a comforting arm around her shoulders. "You're not going to lose your father or your son. Don't even think in those terms."

Pressing her lips together, Lucita tried to ward off the tears that continually burned the back of her eyes.

"You know, Nicci, four months ago I was so happy to come back to the Sandbur. Coming home again filled me with new hope. I truly believed I could start life over and put everything that had happened with Derek behind me. And I thought the ranch would be the very best place for Marti. Being with Gracia and the rest of his family was what he needed—but now—oh, God, bringing him here has—" Shaking her head, she whispered tearfully. "What have I done, Nicci? Why does everything I try to do only cause more problems for me and everyone around me?"

Nicci gave her a gentle shake. "Stop it! Stop it right now! In just a little while you've got to climb into that car with Ripp and if you're not pulled together then you could put him, yourself and Marti in danger. And I don't think you want that."

Shamefaced, Lucita pinched the bridge of her nose and sucked in several bracing breaths. "No. Ripp has been—he's gone above and beyond to help me. And I'm not sure why. I've not—made any sort of commitment to him."

Nicci didn't make an immediate reply and Lucita glanced over at her cousin's face. There was a shrewd expression on her pretty features, as though she could see things that Lucita couldn't.

"Ripp is a dedicated lawman. But I don't think that has anything to do with him wanting to help you and Marti. With or without a commitment from you—he cares. Maybe when this is all over you should think about that."

But when would this ever be over, Lucita wondered sickly. And would Ripp still be around when that time came?

Rising from her seat on the edge of the mattress, she walked over to the dresser and began to pull her long hair into a ponytail.

"The sun is going down," she said in a strained voice. "I'd better get ready to leave."

Chapter Nine

Five miles down Salt Lick Road was a low hill with a wide pull-off decorated with a row of rural mailboxes. It was a lonely spot out in the countryside, a place where a rancher once had a maze of feedlots. Many years ago, the wooden corrals had been torn down. Now the only things left were a windmill, a water tank and a molasses lick for the herd of cattle pastured there.

There were no houses or neighboring structures to be seen for at least two miles surrounding the old salt lick. The only thing suggesting that people lived on the finger roads branching off Salt Lick were the mailboxes. The isolation was no doubt one of the main reasons the kidnapper had specified the place for the money to be dropped. The rough dirt road was hardly traveled and when it was, the dust boiling behind a vehicle was a dead giveaway.

Lucita drove the SUV slowly; her hands white-knuckle, her heart pounding like thunder in her ears. Somewhere in the near vicinity was a group of Rangers and deputies in undercover vehicles, but they were too far away to give her and Ripp any sort of support if things went wrong. Their job was to wait until the kidnapper picked up the money, then nab him as he drove onto one of the main roads.

In the seat next to Lucita were two duffel bags stuffed with five-hundred-dollar bills, straight from one of the Sandbur accounts, along with phony money the Rangers used for just such situations as this. Lucita didn't know exactly how much real money was in the bag, nor did she care. Money had ruined her marriage and now it was being bartered for the life of her son. She hated it.

Behind Lucita the seats of the SUV had been folded down to make a cover for Ripp, who lay flat against the floorboard.

Throughout the drive from the Sandbur to the drop-off point, he'd said very little, except to give her a word of encouragement now and then. But talk hadn't been necessary. Just knowing he was back there was enough to bolster her courage.

"I'm here at the pull-off, Ripp. It's eight o'clock on the dot."

"Do you see anyone? Anything?"

With the motor running, she cut the lights on the vehicle and stared around at the darkness encircling the vehicle. "I can't see much. It looks like nothing but pastureland with a few trees and a small herd of cattle."

"Good," he said in hushed voice. "Lower the windows, then kill the motor and get out of the vehicle.

Start carrying the bags over to the fence—I'll be covering you from the back window."

"All right."

Her hands were shaking almost violently as she gathered up the duffel bags and opened the door. For one second before she stepped to the ground, she wasn't sure her legs would carry her to the jagged-topped cedar post where she was supposed to place the money. But she didn't have a choice. If the kidnapper was close by, he would no doubt open fire on Ripp if she had him come out to help her. And that was a risk she would never let him take.

Sensing her hesitation, Ripp whispered, "Lucita? Can you do this?"

Swallowing at the heartbeat throbbing in her throat, she whispered back, "I'm going. Now."

The distance from the SUV to the fence couldn't have been more than thirty feet, but to Lucita it was the longest walk she'd ever made in her life. Guided only by a sliver of moon, she took one careful step at a time.

Except for the faint sounds of cattle chewing the Bermuda grass and a few buzzing locusts, the night was quiet and still. The humid air was hot and Lucita could feel sweat drenching her face, rolling beneath her blouse and seeping into the waistband of her jeans.

Once she finally reached the fence, she dropped the bags and went down on her knees to search the ground around the cedar post. A note with directions to find Marti was supposed to be here somewhere. But where?

Frantically, she began shoving away small rocks and weeds. Fire ants climbed onto her hand and instantly seared her skin with bites and stings. Biting down on her lip to keep from screaming out, she frantically brushed at the insects while trying to continue on with her search for any sign of a paper.

Where was it? *Oh, God, please let me find it,* Lucita prayed. If she couldn't locate the note, her only choice would be to carry the bags back to the SUV. The money was their only leverage for getting information to find Marti.

She was beginning to think the kidnapper had led them on a wild-goose chase when she decided to give the post a shove. It was loose, and as the base pulled away from the hard ground, she spotted a piece of dark-colored paper sticking up from the edge of the hole.

Snatching it up, she raced to the SUV and jumped inside.

"Damn it, Lucita! You were out there forever! What took so long?"

He sounded shaken and she couldn't blame him. Even though it couldn't have been more than five minutes, it felt as if she'd been out there by the fence for a half an hour. No doubt he'd been expecting shots to ring out at any given moment.

"I couldn't find the note at first. But I've got it now!"

"Give it to me and drive! Quick," he ordered.

She tossed the paper back over the seat to him and quickly started the engine. As she started to pull onto the road, the flash of headlights bounced off the side-view mirror.

"Ripp! There's someone coming!" she yelped out.

"Don't worry about it. Go. Now!"

"But if it's the police they're going to ruin everything!" she cried.

"It's not the police. Now do as I say!"

He barked out the order and she reacted by stomping

on the gas pedal. The tires on the SUV spun in the gravel and the vehicle fishtailed onto the main road.

As she fought with the steering wheel, Ripp vaulted into the passenger seat and quickly punched out a number on his cell phone.

"The money is dropped," he reported bluntly to the person at the other end. "I've got the directions. I'll call you when I figure this thing out."

From the corner of her eye, she could see him snap the phone shut and begin to read the note with a penlight.

Her heart was pounding with fear, yet underneath the awful dread was a wild surge of hope. Marti. They were going to find Marti. They had to.

She was silently repeating that mantra when Ripp spoke. "Keep going in this direction until we reach Willow Point Road."

The headlights behind them were growing dimmer now, telling her that the vehicle wasn't trying to keep up with them. Still, her throat was so tight with nerves, she squeaked when she asked, "How far is that?"

"I know this area. It's not far. Maybe three miles."

"Then what?"

"We turn east and head toward Victoria until we reach—"

Ripp continued to read the note, but Lucita was no longer registering his words. She was envisioning Marti. Finding him. Pulling him into her arms and never letting go.

"—house by the canal."

Catching the end of Ripp's words, she took her eyes off the rough road for one brief second to look at him. "Do you know where that is? Can we find it?"

"I don't know exactly where it is. But we'll damn well find it, Lucita. Right now, just concentrate on driving and I'll tell you when to turn next."

She could do that. For the next fifteen minutes she concentrated on keeping the vehicle between the ditches and following Ripp's orders.

About five miles southwest of Victoria, residences began to appear, but they were few and far between. Eventually, Ripp directed her to turn onto a small blacktopped road that led them past a salvage yard with acres of trashed vehicles. To their left, a ghost yard of broken-down mobile homes were jammed at odd angles on the side of a hill. She caught faint glimpses of busted-out windows, doors hanging open and metal siding falling away to expose hunks of insulation. The idea that Marti might be in one of those dark, rat-filled places made her shiver with fear.

"Ripp, I think we're coming up on the canal. Do you think Marti might be in one of those trailers?"

He glanced from the note in his hand to the junkyard on their left. "I don't know. It just says house by the canal."

As the bridge spanning the canal suddenly appeared, Lucita stomped on the brake and brought the SUV to a halt in the middle of the street.

"What the hell are you doing?" Ripp barked at her.

Breathing hard with fear and frustration, she tossed up her hands. "We're at the canal, Ripp. There's no use going farther!"

"There might be a house on the north side of the canal. Now step on it!"

"But those old trailers—wouldn't they be a likely place to hide someone?"

"We can always turn around and search them later. I'm betting on a regular house."

Realizing he could be right, she gunned the vehicle across the bridge.

"There isn't anything around here, Ripp. No street-lights, no traffic. It's eerie. I—"

"There's another road," he interrupted. "Turn now! To your left!"

She whipped the steering wheel and the vehicle careened onto a dirt drive. In a matter of seconds, the beam of headlights bounced across some sort of structure partially obscured by a massive oak tree and a thick tangle of rose hedge.

"Stop. Turn off your lights!"

Automatically she followed his orders and once he started to exit the vehicle, she moved to follow.

"No!" he whispered loudly, catching her by the shoulder and pinning her back to the seat. "We don't know who might be in there waiting with a gun. You'll stay right here while I make the initial search."

Lucita's instinct was to rip away from his hold and race to the dark house and she strained against his grip. "Ripp, Marti is my son! Let me go!"

Instead of complying with her wishes, his fingers tightened and he paused for one moment to lean his face close to hers.

She was quivering from head to toe, her breaths coming in rapid gulps as he forced her to focus on the dim outline of his features.

"Lucita, use your head! I care about you. I don't want anything happening to you—or to Marti. Now stay put unless you see me signal otherwise. Understand?"

After a few moments his firm voice penetrated her frantic senses and she nodded jerkily.

"I—I'm sorry, Ripp," she whispered. "I'll stay here. Promise."

"Good girl."

He patted her cheek and then he was out of the vehicle and slipping through the shadows in front of her.

From his vantage point behind the rose hedge, Ripp could see the house was little more than a half-rotted frame. Part of the roof had long ago caved in and the windows were vandalized. There was no front door and on one end of the covered porch was a pile of rotting carpet.

Only moments before, he'd called Sheriff Travers to let him know he was going into the structure. He wasn't about to wait for backup. Not if Marti could be inside. And even though Lucita had promised to stay put, he wouldn't be a bit surprised to turn around and see her glued to his back.

Drawing his weapon, he stepped from behind the hedge and crept stealthily to the back of the house. Once he entered the structure, the faint glimmer of moonlight that had been illuminating his way was gone and he was forced to pull out a tiny flashlight.

Pack rats scurried as the wooden boards beneath his boots creaked from his weight. Inside the tiny rooms, the air was stale and so humid he felt as if he were breathing water. Mosquitoes buzzed around his face and made a feast on his arms. Sweat rolled from his temples and into his eyes, but he didn't dare reach up to wipe it away. Not when the next second might find him face-to-face with the barrel of a gun.

Long, long moments passed before Ripp reached the front room of the house. By then it was apparent that the kidnapper wasn't present. But was Marti?

Holstering his weapon, he began to search every dark nook and corner while he prayed for Marti's safety.

"Marti? Marti, are you here?"

He'd hardly gotten the words past his lips when he spotted a closet door with a wooden pallet jammed tightly at an angle between the door handle and the floor.

Flinging it out of the way, Ripp jerked the door open and heaved out an enormous breath of relief as he stared straight at the stunned boy sitting cross-legged on the floor. A patch of gray duct tape covered his mouth.

"Marti!" Dropping to his knees, he carefully pulled the tape from the boy's lips. "Marti, are you okay, son?"

Tears welled up in Marti's eyes and then he flung himself straight into Ripp's arms and began to sob.

Ripp held Lucita's child tightly as an overwhelming sense of protectiveness swept over him. "It's okay, Marti," he said, rubbing a hand over the boy's head. "It's all over. Let's go home."

Later, as the clock neared midnight, Lucita stood in a hallway at the sheriff's department. Her father's arm was wrapped tightly around her shoulders as the two of them stared through a small window and into an interrogation room.

Inside the tiny square space, a slip of a woman sat at a bare table. Her wrists were handcuffed together, her head bent. Red hair hung in limp hanks around her head, hiding most of her face. Across from her sat one of the Rangers who'd been working the case. At the moment he seemed content to let the woman talk at her own pace.

Two hours after Lucita and Ripp had dropped the money at the salt lick, the Rangers had picked the woman up on a rural road east of Goliad. A .38 snub-nosed revolver had been found on her person and another Colt .45 in her vehicle, along with the duffel bags full of money.

Her name was Faye Warner and she was a stranger to Lucita and the whole family.

"Surprised the hell out of me when they brought her in," Mingo muttered. "All along I figured it was Derek."

Lucita swallowed as she tried to control the wild swing of her emotions. Looking at the woman felt surreal, as though she was viewing evil in human form.

"She says that Derek is dead," Lucita said bluntly. "Shot by the Mexican mafia near Cuidad Juarez about a year ago for reneging on a drug deal. And so far her story has checked out with the Mexican police."

Since they'd brought her in for booking, Faye Warner had been singing like a bird in order to gain leniency. Lucita was still in shock to hear that her ex-husband had been having an affair with this woman. That the two of them had stolen her inheritance together and spent it lavishly down on the Mexican coast, living the high life until Derek got mixed up with the wrong people.

Mingo snorted. "Justice, if you ask me. He never knew what he had in you and Marti. All he ever wanted was your money. Well, he got that and more. Only God can help his soul now."

"Ripp said that this woman had been planning the kidnapping for a long time because her money was running low. She'd followed me around in Corpus, memorizing my daily routine and figuring out the best way to nab Marti."

Mingo muttered a few curse words under his breath. "Guess you put a kink in her plans when you moved up here from Corpus."

Lucita nodded numbly. She'd never felt so cold in her life. Even the warmth of her father's hand couldn't keep her from shivering.

"That's when she decided to nix the kidnapping plan for a while. Her running me off the road was meant to scare me enough to simply put the money in the bank account when she asked for it instead of taking the chance of getting caught grabbing Marti. When we didn't comply with her wishes, she finally put the kidnapping plan into action. And all along, this woman had wanted us all to think it was Derek's doing."

"In a way it was," Mingo stated flatly. "He's the one who brought this evil person into our lives."

Lucita's own guilt washed up in her throat like bitter bile. "I should have listened to you, Daddy. All those years ago when you tried to tell me that Derek was no good. I thought you were just being a possessive parent—that no man would have been good enough for your daughter. But you were right all along. And now I feel so stupid. I nearly got my own son killed!"

Tears that seemed unending, once again began to flow down her cheeks. Mingo pulled her head against his shoulder and patted her back just as he had when she'd been a small girl with a big hurt.

"Hush, my little darlin'. This is all over now. You have a new life ahead of you and that's what you need to concentrate on now."

A week later, the heinous ordeal continued to haunt Lucita each time she allowed her mind to drift to all that had happened. As for Marti, the family had tried to soften the details of his father's death and his association with the kidnapper. Even so, they couldn't erase the trauma that her son had been through. He'd not only been held hostage, but he'd had to face the fact that there would never be a chance for Derek to reform or be a part of his family again.

During this past week, she'd kept Marti home from school. He'd gone to counseling with the family priest and also a child therapist. Both professionals had told Lucita that her son was dealing with the whole experience in an open and healthy way, yet she couldn't help but worry. She could see the somber sadness in his eyes and her heart ached for him. She wished she could wave a wand and make him instantly happy. But the only thing that seemed to put a smile on his face for now was Ripp.

The night the deputy had pulled Marti from the closet in that dilapidated house, her son had clung to him and refused to leave his side. After Faye's initial booking and interrogation Ripp had ended up spending the remainder of that night on the couch in order to make Marti feel safe. And since then, Ripp had been out to the ranch every day to check on the boy. The two of them had taken to playing catch in the backyard with Marti's baseball and last evening they'd walked down to the horse barn to visit Trampus. Clearly, her son was growing closer and closer to Ripp. And there was no denying that she was growing completely attached to the man.

That afternoon Lucita was in the mudroom, loading the washer with dirty clothes when she heard voices entering the kitchen.

Glancing around the doorjamb, she saw Ripp dressed in jeans and a green checked shirt being tugged across the kitchen floor by her son. Yesterday Ripp had warned her that he would probably show up at some point this evening to check on Marti and she'd agreed that right now he seemed to be the best medicine for her son. But she wondered if he realized just what his visits were doing to her. Just hearing his voice filled her heart with sunshine.

"Mom! Ripp is here!" Marti called out with loud excitement.

Stepping into the kitchen, Lucita smiled at Ripp as she smoothed a hand over her mussed hair.

"Yes, I see. And as loud as you were yelling everyone over in the big house probably knows Ripp is here, too," she teased Marti.

Wrinkling his nose at his mother, Marti snatched a hold on Ripp's arm and tugged him toward the back door. "C'mon, Ripp, I wanta show you the rattlesnake that Grandpa killed! It has ten rattlers and he's gonna use the skin to make a hatband for me."

"Marti," Lucita called as her son continued to pull Ripp along. "Ripp has only walked in the door. He might like to sit down for a minute before you start dragging him all over the ranch."

"Aw, Mom, Ripp ain't old," Marti shot back. "He don't get tired."

Above the boy's head, Ripp grinned and winked at Lucita. "No, Mom, I don't get tired. You go on with what you were doing and we'll be back in a little while."

Lucita waved them out the door. Once she was certain they were away from the house, she raced to the bedroom and quickly stripped off her sloppy house-cleaning clothes. After jerking on a pair of white shorts and a red-and-white tropical print blouse, she dashed on light makeup and brushed her hair into a loose fall of waves upon her shoulders.

As she looked at herself in the mirror, she realized it had been years since she'd felt this excited about anything. Just the thought of being with Ripp made her giddy. And though she realized she was behaving foolishly, she couldn't help herself. Ripp made her feel like a woman again. He made her feel attractive and wanted. Something she desperately needed after having her self-esteem squashed by Derek.

By the time Ripp and Marti returned to the guest-house, Lucita had made a pitcher of lemonade and the three of them sat on the patio drinking the iced drinks and eating homemade cookies.

Marti was telling Ripp all about the trails on the ranch where they could ride horses when Gracia walked over from the big house to join them.

After kissing both Lucita and Ripp on the cheek, the teenager turned an impish grin on her little cousin. "Hey, Marti, I'm going to a roller-skating party tonight. Want to come along?"

Marti glanced thoughtfully from Ripp to his cousin as though he wasn't at all sure he wanted to leave his buddy.

"I don't know," he mumbled. "When are you goin'?"

Like her dad, Gracia was a tough little cookie and didn't believe in coddling her cousin for any reason. Once Marti had been rescued, the girl had hugged him and fussed over him for about two hours and then she'd gone back to giving him orders.

Rolling her eyes with impatience now, she tossed her head. "In thirty minutes. So get up and get ready. A friend of mine has rented the whole rink for the evening and there will be all kinds of food to eat. You know you want to go. And when we get back, you can stay all night in the big house. I've got a new video game we can play."

Once again, Ripp could feel Marti turning a questioning look on him and for one brief moment he almost felt like a father to the boy.

"What would you do if you were me, Ripp?"

Ripp chuckled. "Well, I'll put it this way, Marti. If a pretty girl asked me to a party, I don't think I'd disappoint her."

Marti tossed a comical frown at Gracia while he said to Ripp, "Aw, Gracia is my cousin. She's not like a girlfriend."

Ripp chuckled again. "Yeah. But she's good company, isn't she? And I'll see you soon."

Rising to his feet, Marti glanced earnestly at him. "Promise?"

Touched by the almost-pleading sound in Marti's voice, Ripp nodded. "I promise. Now go have a good time. That is, if your mother gives you permission to go."

"Oh, you will, won't you?" Gracia asked Lucita. "I'll keep a close watch on him this time. I promise. Please, please."

Realizing that Gracia needed to know she could be trusted with Marti's welfare just as much as her son needed the outing, Lucita wasn't about to deny either child.

"Of course Marti can go," she said.

Excited now, Marti waved for his cousin to join him in the house. "C'mon, Gracia, help me get my things ready."

A few minutes later, the children had raced over to the big house, leaving Lucita and Ripp alone on the patio.

For the past week, since Ripp had been coming daily to the house, Marti had always been present. Now that her son was gone, Lucita was keenly aware of the sexual tension building between them.

"Well, this is—I wasn't expecting this to happen." Rising from her chair, she began to cover the container of cookies with a plastic lid. "Do you think letting him go was the right thing to do?"

"The very best thing to do," he answered quickly.

Turning, she darted a glance at him. "I think so, too. Good for him and Gracia. But I—I can't help but think about the last time I let Marti go for an outing. I thought—" She broke off with a shudder. "I was afraid I'd never see my son alive again."

Instantly Ripp was on his feet, wrapping his arms around her shoulders and pulling her against him. "Lucita, you're going to think about that night probably for the rest of your life. But you also know that you can't keep Marti confined because you're afraid."

With a shake of her head, she murmured, "I'm not afraid, Ripp. Not now. Maybe that sounds crazy, but getting Marti back, learning that Derek is dead—I don't know, it's like the terrible cloud that's been following me has disappeared and I can finally see sunshine again. Does that make sense?"

Placing his forefinger beneath her chin, he lifted her face up to his. "It makes all the sense in the world." He brushed his fingertips against her cheek. "And now that we're alone, I'm wondering if you'd like to have dinner with me tonight."

Surprise flickered in her eyes and then she laughed softly. "Dinner? Am I cooking?"

"No. I am. At my place. I'd like for you to see it, Lucita. It's nothing fancy, but it's mine."

Just standing in the circle of his arms, the front of his body pressing against hers, was enough to make Lucita's heart pound, her blood heat with excitement. Kissing him in the gazebo had been days ago, yet the memory of those moments still burned deep within Lucita, reminding her of what could have been or maybe what could be.

"I'd love to see your place."

He smiled, but just as quickly the warm expression faded and his eyes went somber. "Lucita—before we go. I—there's something I want to say. About me being here—a part of the reason is Marti. I care about him very much. But he's not the only reason I've been turning up every day. Or maybe I'm wasting my breath here. Maybe you already knew that."

The husky suggestion in his voice turned her bones to mush and her lips quivered as she smiled shyly up at him. "What I know is that Marti needs you. And so do I."

A long breath of relief rushed from him and then his head lowered slowly toward hers. Anticipating his kiss, Lucita snuggled closer and closed her eyes.

"No," Ripp said suddenly. "Can't do it. If I kiss you now I have a feeling we'll never get away from here."

Lucita's eyes flew open just as he grabbed her hand and began tugging her toward the house. "Ripp!" she exclaimed with a laugh. "Are we in *that* much of a hurry?"

He paused long enough to toss her a seductive grin. "Yeah. I'm in a great big hurry to make love to you."

Chapter Ten

On the way to Ripp's place, Lucita tried not to think about his comment. Make love to her? Had he meant that literally? Just thinking of being connected to Ripp in such an intimate way was enough to curl her toes. She found it very hard to think about anything else as they drove toward Goliad.

But when he finally turned down a short dirt lane and pulled to a stop in front of a wood-sided house, she was suddenly piqued with curiosity. This was Ripp's home. It was an important part of him and she was eager to see everything.

The house and nearby garage were white, trimmed with green. The house was built in long, shotgun style with a porch running across the front. Several Chinese Pistache trees, slash pines and one enormous pecan tree shaded the structure, while at one end of the porch a huge oleander bush dripped with white blossoms.

"Sorry the grass is a little long," he said as he helped her to the ground. "I've been too busy to mow."

"Oh, don't apologize. It all looks very pretty to me."

His short laugh held a hint of disbelief. "Thanks for that, Lucita. But let's face it, this place is—well, it's nothing compared to what you have."

Lucita laughed. "Ripp, I don't have a home of my own right now! I'm living in my father's guesthouse. That's what I have. So quit comparing and show me around."

A crooked grin slashed his face. "Yeah, you're right, you're homeless," he teased. "And I don't have one damn thing to apologize for."

As both of them laughed, he placed his hand against her back and urged her toward the house. Before they reached the steps, a black Labrador came racing from across the yard, barking with excitement. He ran straight to Lucita, reared up on his hind legs and pawed the air.

"Don't you dare jump on our guest, Chester!" Ripp gently warned the dog. "I'll lock you in your pen."

Seeming to understand that threat, Chester bounced down on all fours and whined. Laughing, Lucita reached out and stroked the dog's head.

"Chester, you're just too handsome. Marti would love you."

As the shiny-coated dog wiggled and shivered against her legs, Ripp said, "Chester would love Marti, too. I don't play nearly enough to suit him."

"Will he fetch?"

Ripp quickly placed a finger against his lips in a shushing gesture. "Lord help us, don't say that word! He has a piece of rawhide—"

Before Ripp could finish, the dog leaped away from them and disappeared around the side of the house.

Bemused by the dog's behavior, she looked at Ripp. "What's wrong? Why did he leave?"

"He heard you say *fetch*. He's gone after his bone— or what used to be a bone. Now it's just a piece of chewed-up leather. Maybe we'd better go in the house before he gets back."

Reaching for her hand, Ripp tugged her toward the steps, but Lucita dug her heels in the thick carpet of grass.

"I'm not about to disappoint Chester. Besides, I want to see the rest of the yard before we go in."

Groaning with amused indulgence he threw up his hands in surrender. "That dog is more than a nuisance. He's—"

"Back," Lucita interrupted with a laugh as Chester skidded to a stop between her and Ripp. A nasty piece of leather was hanging from his mouth.

The dog dropped the treasure at Lucita's feet. Laughing, she picked it up and threw the rawhide chew to a far corner of the yard. As Chester raced after it, Ripp curled his arm around her shoulders.

"I think he's already fallen in love with you."

The three of them made their way around the back of the house and while Chester patiently waited to fetch again, Ripp showed Lucita a small outbuilding that he called his workshop. The area was equipped with a table saw, drill press, work counter and a vast array of carpentry tools. Outside, on a small, redbrick patio, he pointed to a fancy, shingle-roofed doghouse that he'd constructed for Chester and then to the many purple martin houses resting atop a row of tall poles lining the backyard fence.

The birdhouses were equally ornate, all of them done in three-story Creole style, right down to the black iron balustrades on the tiny porches.

Learning that Ripp was such an accomplished carpenter surprised Lucita, but even more unexpected was the vegetable garden growing in a sunny spot some distance away from the house.

Presently, the patch of ground was still yielding squash, okra and a few late-summer tomatoes. The okra stalks were at least ten feet tall, soaring above the enormous sunflowers that grew at the garden's edge.

With her hands on her slim hips, Lucita stood surveying the vegetable patch. "Ripp, I'm so amazed. I never figured you to be a man of the soil."

His smile crooked, he lazily tangled a finger in her light brown hair. "What did you think I was?" he teased softly. "Just a gun-totin' lawman?"

Trying not to outwardly shiver from his sensual touch, she looked away from him and out to the green sweep of land dotted with spreading live oaks. "No. I didn't think that." She glanced curiously up at him. "I guess I haven't had much time to think of anything except how to keep my family safe." The corners of her lips tilted upward. "But now I'm getting to see a part of you that I didn't know about and I—like it."

To her surprise a faint flush spread over his face. "Lucita, growing a few vegetables doesn't take special skills."

She frowned at him. "I wouldn't say that. Not just anyone can make things grow like this. I certainly wouldn't know how. Nor can anyone build the sort of houses you made for Chester or the purple martins. Where did you learn these skills?"

"From my dad. Remember, I told you he was a farmer before he ever became Goliad County sheriff. And he was pretty handy with a hammer and saw, too. He wasn't the sort that hired helped to do anything that needed doing around the farm. He did it himself. I guess some of it rubbed off on me."

She smiled up at him. "Well, I'm notably impressed."

It was downright crazy how much power this woman had over him, Ripp thought. Just a smile from her was enough to make him feel as though he was walking ten inches off the ground. Being near her injected him with joy and almost made him forget that he was exposing his heart. Something that he'd vowed to never do again after Pamela had walked out on him.

"Does your brother share your talents?" she asked.

Her question diverted his thoughts and he chuckled lightly. "Mac? No. Mac thinks I'm boring. He's into raising cattle and raising hell on the side—if you know what I mean."

She looked amused as she pondered this revelation. "I see. In other words, you're nothing like your brother."

Laughing outright, he looped his arm around hers and turned her toward the house. "God, I must really be boring. I'd better feed you some supper before you fall asleep."

A suggestive smile slanted her lips and Ripp felt a fire flicker deep in his belly.

"I really doubt I'm going to get *that* bored," she gently teased.

Once inside Ripp's kitchen, Lucita insisted that a light meal was all they needed and he complied by making a plateful of tacos, along with guacamole and tortilla chips.

After the two of them had eaten, they went out to the

front porch and sat on the wooden swing hanging at one end. The night was still very balmy with just enough southerly breezes to keep most of the mosquitoes away. Chester was curled in a black ball at her feet and Ripp's arm was circled around her shoulders. Lucita couldn't remember a time that she'd felt this content.

Sighing, she said, "This is so peaceful, Ripp."

"Well, compared to the Sandbur, this place is very quiet. I don't have any close neighbors and no one is ever around here except for me. Sometimes Mac shows up for a visit, but that's about it."

His upper body was pressing against her arm and part of her back. The hard warmth of him was both comforting and exciting and several times during the past few minutes she'd had to fight with herself to keep from turning her head and pressing her lips to his.

"That's not a bad thing," Lucita told him. "Frankly, I've had enough excitement this past month to last me a lifetime."

The fingers resting against her shoulder began to entwine in her hair, stroking the long strands lying against her skin. In response, her breathing slowed and her heart picked up its pace.

"I think Marti is doing incredibly well for all he's been through," he said. "Your son is a strong boy, Lucita. You should be proud."

"I am." Turning her head slightly, she lifted her gaze to his. "And I'm very grateful to you, Ripp, for all that you've done for him. You've become his hero, you know."

He grimaced. "I'm not a hero, Lucita. I only rescued him from a closet. Anyone could have done that."

"Rescued. That's the way Marti looks at it. When you entered that old house by the canal, you had no idea where the kidnapper might be. She could have been hidden in one of the rooms, waiting to ambush you. You put yourself in danger to find him. Don't make light of what you've done for him, Ripp."

Shrugging, he said, "Well, I'd rather be Marti's friend than his hero. That's how I feel about it."

A soft laugh passed her lips. "Don't worry. You're all that and more to my son."

He quietly digested her comment before he spoke again. "You know, the first time I met Marti I got the feeling he didn't much like me. He was a little stand-offish. Obviously something changed his mind."

Lucita nodded. "That evening when he first spotted you in the kitchen with me I think…he got the impression that you were there for reasons that had nothing to do with your job. And—well—for the past three years Marti didn't want any man trying to replace the spot in his heart that he'd always reserved for his father. I believe that all along, despite what he said, my son was hoping and praying Derek would come back to us, that his father would eventually show up as a better person and want to resume his spot in the family. Now Marti understands his wish will never come true and I—" Her expression troubled, she shifted on the swing so that she was facing Ripp head-on. "I'm afraid he's beginning to see you as a…father figure, Ripp."

Slowly his hand lifted to cup the side of her face and it was all Lucita could do to keep from groaning aloud as the warmth of his touch filled her with sweet pleasure.

"Have you ever stopped to think that I might be seeing him as a son?"

It was the very last thing she'd expected him to say and for long moments all she could do was stare at him.

Finally, she managed to whisper, "I'm afraid to ask what that means."

Leaning earnestly forward, he wrapped his hands around her upper arms. "Don't you know, Lucita?" he asked, his voice raw and husky. "Can't you see how I feel about you? I've fallen in love with you. I want to be a part of your life. Yours and Marti's."

Tentatively, wondrously, she touched her fingertips to his cheeks. He loved her? For so long after Derek had disappeared, she'd thought of herself as incapable of holding on to any man's interest. It seemed too incredible to believe that Ripp saw her differently.

"Ripp, you don't really know me," she tried to reason. "And you—"

"How can you say that?" he interrupted. "This past month I've watched you handle a horrid situation with more courage than most people will ever show over a lifetime. I know what you're made of, Lucita. But then, I think I knew what sort of woman you were long before Marti was kidnapped."

Inside she was leaping with joy, shouting that this wonderful man loved her—loved her in spite of the mistakes she'd made in the past. How could she resist him, resist the very thing she needed the most? She couldn't. It was that simple.

Resting her forehead against his, she said, "Ripp, from the first moment we met—you frightened me."

Easing back from her, he asked with puzzlement, "Frightened you?"

Her fingers flattened against his cheek, then cupped his strong jaw. "Yes, because you woke up something inside me. For the first time in years I was looking at a man—at you—in a sexual way. And since then, each time we're together I feel something pushing and pulling between us. And it scares me, Ripp. I—"

"Oh, no, sweetheart," he broke in with whispered words. "Don't be scared of me—of this attraction between us. Just let me show you how I feel. Let me love you."

The tenderness in his hands, the seduction of his gravelly voice, fueled her need to be in his arms. With a tiny moan of surrender, she pressed her lips against his.

Instantly Ripp took control of the kiss, devouring her lips with a hunger that yanked the very breath from her body. Mindlessly, she opened her mouth to accept his tongue while her hands explored his face, the strong column of his neck and the long-muscled slope of his shoulders.

Heat spiraled through her, caught her senses and swirled them into hazy cloud. Beneath her thin blouse, she could feel her nipples tightening, her breasts aching for the touch of his hands.

Trying to draw even closer together, their bodies shifted and the swing rocked wildly. Planting his boot against the planked porch, Ripp stopped the violent pitch long enough to draw both of them out of the swing and to their feet.

"Come on," he whispered. "Let's go inside."

Stepping over a sleeping Chester, he led her into the dimly lit house and didn't stop until they were standing in a bedroom full of shadows. As Lucita darted a glance at the double bed, she shivered.

Ripp must have felt the tiny tremors rushing through her because he paused long enough to look at her.

"You can change your mind, you know."

His voice was thick with desire and she realized with

shocking clarity that if she decided to walk away at this moment everything between them would end. If common sense was dictating her movements, then she might pull away from the light hold he had on her arm. But as she looked up at his rugged face, the only thing she felt was her heart beating fast, begging to be one with this man.

"I don't want to change my mind. I—oh, Ripp, you're what I want!"

With a groan of triumph, Ripp reached for her and once his lips had pressed a foray of kisses over her face, he began to peel away her clothing and then his own.

When his body was finally revealed to her eager gaze, Lucita was instantly captivated with the hard, smooth muscles stretching across his chest and abdomen, down his long arms and legs. He was a man of strength, a man who undeniably wanted her and just the sight of his desire made her desperate to touch him, to absorb his hard arousal.

After another long, consuming kiss, Ripp laid her crosswise on the bed, then stretched himself alongside her. As his hand kneaded one pale breast, he mouthed against her cheek, "Do I need to get protection?"

Reaching for his shoulder, she urged him toward her while assuring him that she was safe on that count.

"Now you're probably thinking I'm taking oral contraceptives just to be prepared for…something like this," she said awkwardly. Even though it shouldn't matter, the idea of Ripp thinking of her as a promiscuous woman bothered her greatly. "But the truth is, Ripp, that—oh, this is embarrassing—"

"Oh, honey, I don't want you to be embarrassed. I want you to be able to say anything to me. Anything."

"I've only made love to one man in my life before now."

Groaning, he buried his face against the curve of her throat and murmured, "Tonight both of us are going to forget the past, Lucita. From this moment on it's only you and me. The two of us together. That's all that matters."

Lifting his head, his hot gaze slowly feasted on the delicate features of her face, lingered on the small mounds of her breasts, then moved on to peruse the indention of her waist and the valley below it. And then his hands began to move, wandering, inspecting, skimming over her body like flames racing over dry tinder.

"Damn, but you're beautiful, Lucita. Every inch of you. You look like a painting. All pink and brown. Smooth and sweet." His hand slipped beneath one leg and drew it upward until her knee was within reach of his lips. He kissed her kneecap and the curve of her calf before his mouth directed its ministrations toward her inner thigh.

The slow wet progress of his mouth marched upward until Lucita was spinning violently in a dark, heated haze. Desire was the only axle holding her together and if he didn't ease the pressure pounding through her body, she was going to fly completely apart.

Snaring her fingers in his thick hair, she lifted his head just enough to see his face.

"Ripp, don't tease me," she choked out. "Come here. I can't wait. Let me feel you inside me."

With a growl of compliance, he quickly positioned himself over her and entered her with one, smooth thrust.

The instant connection took Lucita's breath away, and then fiery sparks of pleasure showered through her body, sizzling every nerve ending. The sensation was so incredible that Lucita actually cried out in shock.

Above her, Ripp clenched his jaw and moaned. Lucita recognized that he was fighting to keep this time between them going forever. And even then, forever wouldn't be long enough. Not for her.

"Oh, my lovely," he whispered. "My lovely Lucita."

Through crescents of thick lashes, Lucita watched a myriad of emotions sweeping across his face. The tender hunger she saw among them filled her heart with an emotion too big to understand.

Unbearable need overtook her and wrapping her arms around him, she thrust her hips upward. That sole movement fractured the moment and ignited a firestorm between them. Hunger and need exploded, fed the mindless surge of their bodies.

Like a horse racing wild and free over the open plains, Lucita felt everything inside her rushing forward, seeking, straining to find that exquisite spot where the hot sun would melt her bones, where she and Ripp could float and drift on a sea of grass.

Time ceased to exist for Lucita. Yet she was somehow able to recognize the end was coming all too soon. She tried to stop the final ascent, tried to clench back the sweet sensations shivering through her. But they were too strong and her body too weak to resist the delights he was giving her. Gripping his shoulders, she sought his mouth and let herself soar.

The deep moans in her throat, the tight clench of her body fueled Ripp to join her in that climb to paradise and seconds later he was crying out her name, clutching her small frame to him as he drove his seed deep, deep inside her.

Ripp wasn't sure how much time had passed when he finally became aware of Lucita's small body lying limply beneath him. With his breathing still ragged, his heart pounding to the point of explosion, he somehow managed to ease his weight from her and roll to his side.

Once his breathing quieted and his rocked senses settled back to earth, he reached for her and tucked her damp body in the curve of his.

As he stroked her moist hair off her forehead, he searched for the right words to speak to her, but a drunken man would have had more vocabulary than he seemed to possess at the moment. Even so, how could mere words convey what he was feeling? he wondered. She'd taken his body, his heart on a wild trip, one from which he'd still not totally returned.

Shutting his eyes, he allowed his hand to glide over the curve of her hip and linger against her thigh. Next to his chest, he could feel the rise and fall of her breasts as she breathed and the closeness of her intoxicated him.

Pushing the tangled mass of hair away from her shoulder, he bent his head and kissed the sheen of sweat glistening along her collarbone.

"Was that a smile I saw on your lips?" she whispered drowsily.

Her hand fell limply against his arm. He lifted it, pressed kisses to her fingers, then turned her palm up and tasted the center.

"Right now I think I'll go on smiling forever," he uttered like a blissful fool.

Enfolding her hand in his, he turned his attention to her face. Her brown eyes were soft, her lips curved in a gentle smile. At that moment he knew that even if he lived to be an old man, he'd never see a more beautiful woman than this one now cradled in his arms.

"I'm glad you're happy."

His chuckles fanned her cheeks. "Happy? Woman, just give me the chance and I could jump over the moon."

Laughing softly, Lucita glanced toward the curtained window. "I'm not sure the moon has risen yet. Maybe I'd better go out on the porch and look."

One arm tightened around her. "I'm not letting you go anywhere. Not tonight," he growled.

Even though his possessive attitude thrilled Lucita, it also reminded her that she had more than herself to think about and she looked at him with dismay. "Ripp! I can't stay here all night! Marti—"

"Is staying the night with Gracia. Remember? I'm sure after their late night, he won't wake early. I promise to have you home before daylight."

Relaxing somewhat, she slanted him a wry grin. "Oh, that's great. A woman of my age coming home at daylight. Are you trying to turn me into a brazen woman?"

He grunted with amusement and then his whole demeanor took on a serious note as he stroked fingertips against the curve of her cheek. "No. I'm trying to turn you into *my* woman."

Closing her eyes, a contented sigh rose up from deep inside to slip past her lips. "I think you've already done that, Ripp."

"No. I mean more than making love to you, Lucita. I want—I want us to be married, Lucita. I want you to be my wife."

Her eyes flew open; her jaw fell. Was he serious? Surely he wasn't, but everything about his earnest expression said otherwise.

"Married? I—Ripp, I don't know what to say! This is—it's so sudden. We've not known each other that long."

"I wasn't aware there was a set time for a person to get to know someone. If there is, I think we can safely say we've surpassed it. Especially now," he added with a wicked grin.

Rising up on one elbow, she stared at him as though he'd just turned into a stranger.

"You really *are* serious," she murmured.

He frowned at her. "Of course I'm serious. I wouldn't joke about something like this."

Rising to a sitting position, she thrust both hands into her hair, then held her head as though it was about to burst. "You're not thinking clearly, Ripp."

Pushing his upper body off the mattress, he rested his hand against her back. "Why?"

Did he actually expect her to give him a simple answer to that question, Lucita wondered incredibly. How could she explain? His proposal had thrilled her with joy, yet it also terrified her, filled her with doubts that hovered over her heart like dark storm clouds.

"Because you don't know what sort of wife I'd be. And I don't—well, when you mentioned your broken relationship you more or less admitted that you haven't been looking for a wife or even considering having a family. A man doesn't take that much of a U-turn in just a matter of days."

His forefinger slipped lazily up and down her backbone, sending flickers of heat over her damp skin. Just the thought of having this man beside her, to make love to her, to hold and comfort her, was all that she could ever dream of. But would he stick around once the passion of the moment cooled? Would she be a fool to think that he would?

"I wasn't looking for a woman, period," he conceded. "But you came along and made me do more than just a U-turn, Lucita. You have me thinking about things—planning things that I never thought I'd want in my life."

Shifting to a sitting position upon the mattress, he pulled her into the circle of his arms. Lucita couldn't resist pillowing her cheek on his strong shoulder.

"Ripp," she began doubtfully. "It's only been a few days since I found out my ex-husband is dead. I need time to absorb all that's happened and—"

His hand tangled in her hair and lifted her head up to his. Lucita had never felt more exposed as his gaze bored deeply into hers.

"Are you still in love with him?"

She shuddered at the thought. "No. That ended a long time ago—when I received his divorce papers in the mail."

"Then what are you trying to say? That you don't care about me?"

How could he even think that after what had just transpired between them, she wondered. She'd poured her heart out to him. She'd allowed him to be inside of her, see inside of her. Because she *loved* him. Only because she loved him.

The sudden realization of her feelings hit her hard. And so did the doubts. Maybe Ripp did care deeply for her right now. But how would he feel after a few months? A few years? When they'd first married, she'd believed Derek loved her. She'd believed their marriage was solid. His desertion had been like a giant earthquake and once the pieces of her shattered life had settled, her self-esteem was nowhere to be found. For the past three years she'd been searching for it, trying to tell herself that she wasn't the reason her husband had left, that she was worthy of a man's love. But she wasn't yet convinced that she was brave enough to try again, to put her complete trust in another man.

"Oh, Ripp, I do care for you. Very much. I wouldn't have—I wouldn't be here with you like this if I didn't care," she tried to explain. "But marriage is a huge step. For right now I think—well, I think it would be best if we…kept our relationship to…that of lovers."

As soon as the words passed her lips, she could feel his whole body tense and withdraw from her, as though it had suddenly dawned on him that she was a woman he didn't really know.

"Lovers." He repeated the word as though he was rolling the taste of it around in his mouth and wasn't finding it particularly palatable. "That's hardly the same as man and wife."

Easing back from him, she saw his blue eyes were full of hurt. The sight tightened her throat, making it difficult to breathe. "No. Not exactly," she huskily agreed. "But we would be together. And it would give us— me—time to think about the future."

Time. Of course she needed time. The practical side of Ripp understood that he was rushing her. But he'd hoped that she was as in love with him as he was with her, that she was straining at the bit to be his wife as much as he was raring to be her husband. Obviously she wasn't feeling anywhere near the devotion he felt toward her. The realization left him feeling as though he'd just been abandoned in a dry desert without any hope for a drink of water.

Time was something Pamela had asked for, but a stack of calendar days hadn't fixed their relationship, he remembered. And once his mother, Frankie, had walked out of his and Mac's young lives, time had done nothing to bring her back or make her decide that she actually loved or wanted her children. If Lucita didn't want to marry him now, time would hardly change her mind.

"Yeah," he said, his voice shadowed with disappointment. "I understand. Marriage is serious. You don't want to leap in without thinking." The way he just had, he thought glumly.

She continued to study his face and Ripp hoped she couldn't see how much she'd just crushed him. If he was going to survive, he needed a little pride to keep him afloat.

"You say you understand," she said quietly, "But I get the feeling that you're—upset with me."

Moving away from her, he swung his legs over the side of the bed and reached for his jeans. As he stood and tugged them up over his naked hips, he said, "No. I'm not upset." He did his best to chuckle, to prove to her and himself that he was as happy as a toad in a summer downpour. "Why would I be? A beautiful woman is sitting naked in my bed. I'd be crazy to be upset."

"Then why are you putting your clothes on?" she questioned.

Glancing over his shoulder, he saw that a puzzled frown marked her forehead.

Why was he pulling on his jeans? Ripp wondered. Any sane, red-blooded man wouldn't leave a sexy, willing woman alone in his bed. But once she'd brushed his marriage proposal to some murky place in the far-off future, making love to her had taken on a different light. It didn't mean the same thing and the realization jarred him like the hard shake of his father's disciplining hand. The special commitment and devotion he'd felt when he'd taken her into his arms had all been one-sided.

Maybe, like her, he needed time, too. To figure out how long his heart could live on nothing but hope.

"I—I've decided you were right," he told her, each word rasping against his throat like a piece of barbed wire. "It wouldn't look very good for either of us if I took you back to the Sandbur at daylight. We'd better start back pretty soon."

Pulling his eyes away from her, he stared into the dark shadows of the bedroom and as he pulled up the zipper on his jeans, he could hear the rustle of her movements on the bed.

After a moment Ripp realized that she was gathering up her clothes from where he'd tossed them only minutes earlier. How fleeting that ecstasy had been, he thought. Earlier, he'd been soaring like a bird, but it hadn't taken him long to fall flat.

"If that's what you want," she said, her voice muffled as she tugged her top over her head.

God, no. It wasn't what he wanted. He wanted to take her into his arms, make love to her over and over. He wanted to hold on to her. Like any man wanted to hold on to the thing he loved the most.

Was this the way his father had felt when he'd watched his beloved wife slowly slipping from his fingers?

Reaching for his shirt, he cleared his throat. "I, uh, just remembered I have something to do early in the morning. We'll get together again. Soon."

Suddenly she was standing in front of him and Ripp felt his heart melting all over again as she placed her palm against the middle of his chest.

"Ripp, whatever you're thinking, just know that you and tonight are special to me."

Special. Was that the same as love? He looked down at the floor and let out a long, heavy breath. "Well, it's like you said, we need time to see what happens."

Chapter Eleven

The Cattle Call Café was a country-style restaurant located in downtown Goliad, a short distance away from the courthouse. The interior was a long rectangular room with a high ceiling fitted with a number of bladed fans to stir the smoke of cooking grease and cigarettes that mingled with the twangy country tunes coming from a radio.

A long bar lined with swiveling stools crossed one end of the room, while the remaining area was fitted with round wooden tables and chairs. The walls were plastered with historical photos and paintings depicting the local area, some of them going as far back as Colonel Fannin's battle at Coleto Creek during the Texas war for Independence.

The café had long been a gathering place for towns-folk, local ranchers and lawmen. Down through the years, Ripp had enjoyed many meals here with his father and brother. He'd sat with Sheriff Travers and his fellow deputies as they'd gobbled down hurried lunches or sometimes were even forced to race away before their plates were ever placed upon the table.

On most days when his work allowed him to stay in town, Ripp ate lunch at the Cattle Call and sometimes had dinner there in the evenings when he wanted to treat himself to a good steak. But this evening he'd not entered the restaurant to treat himself. This evening he wanted to avoid going home to an empty house. He didn't want to remember how it had felt to eat at the kitchen table with Lucita sitting across from him. He didn't want to imagine her smiling face or how just having her in the house had made it feel special.

Damn it, for the past week since he'd made love to the woman of his dreams, it had been a struggle to get his mind to focus on anything other than her. A hundred times he'd wanted to pick up the phone and punch in her number. He wanted to hear her say she was as eager to see him again as he was to see her. He wanted to hear her confess that she loved him and couldn't live another day without him. But the only time that ever happened was in his dreams.

"Thank God. I was about to decide I'd lost my tracking skills. I've been calling your cell phone for the past two hours and looking all over the place for you. I finally thought to look in here."

At the sound of his brother's voice, Ripp glanced up to see a smiling Mac pulling out the chair next to him.

Ripp grunted out a greeting. "Probably because you got hungry."

"Have you already ordered?" Mac asked as a young waitress approached their table.

"Yeah. Catfish and hush puppies."

"I'll have the same, sugar." He gave the waitress a wink, then added, "and about a gallon of sweet tea to go with it."

The petite brunette smiled at Mac as she scribbled words on her order pad, then swished away from the table. Ripp rolled his eyes toward the ceiling. If he possessed half of his brother's sex appeal Lucita would probably be sitting here beside him with a wedding band on her finger.

"What are you doing here?" he asked.

Mac frowned. "What the hell kind of question is that? Every time I show up, you ask me what I'm doing. I'm going to have supper with my brother. That's what I'm doing."

"Sorry if I sounded short. It's just not your normal routine to show up around here on a Saturday night. Didn't you have something better to do?"

"Than see my brother? No."

The waitress returned with Mac's glass of iced sweet tea. Ripp watched the two of them exchange coy glances before she finally turned and headed over to another table.

"Maybe you should ask her out," Ripp suggested, his tone sardonic. "She's certainly giving you all the right signals."

Mac grinned. "Aw, that's just a little minor flirtation, brother. She's got a boyfriend."

"How do you know that?"

"She told me. The first time I asked her out."

Mac laughed as though he found the situation more than funny. But when Ripp didn't join him, his expression sobered.

"What's the matter, brother? You ought to know when I'm joking."

He felt awful about his strained situation with Lucita, but he hardly knew what to do about fixing his state of mind. "I guess I just don't find anything about women amusing just now."

"Oh. Well, they sure as hell aren't to be taken seriously. If you ever let that happen, then you're in trouble. Brenna taught me that much."

Mac's comment reminded Ripp that he wasn't the only McCleod who'd been hurt by a woman. It had taken Mac years to get over his divorce. And then there was their father, Owen, and their mother, Frankie. She'd simply left their father with two young sons. Another man had turned her head and she'd never looked back. As far as Ripp knew, his mother had not once acknowledged the family she'd left behind in any way ever since. It was almost as if the woman had died. And as far as Ripp was concerned, she was dead.

Fiddling with the handle on his coffee cup, he said, "Yeah, I guess she did."

Mac took a long drink of iced tea, then glanced at Ripp over the rim of his glass. "I went by the Dry Gulch. The Cotton Pickers are playing tonight. I thought you might be there enjoying yourself. You deserve it after the long hours you put in on that Sanchez case."

Long hours with Lucita, he thought. Long hours of watching the agony she'd gone through and desperately wanting to make everything right for her. He'd fallen in love with her along the way and for some idiotic reason he'd believed she'd reciprocated that love.

"I wasn't in the mood for music," Ripp glumly replied.

"Humph," Mac grunted with amusement. "What about drinking and dancing?"

Releasing a long sigh, Ripp propped his elbows on the table and leaned toward his brother. "I'm not in the mood for that, either. But you don't need my company to go have a little fun."

The glower on Mac's face said he was getting peeved with Ripp's negative attitude.

"I wasn't asking you to go with me. I'm a big boy. I can go out on the town at night without you watching over me. I might get into a little trouble, but what the hell. A man that always plays it safe might as well be dead." He turned a narrow eye on Ripp. "By the way, you look like you're headed toward the cemetery yourself. What's the matter? Been off your feed?"

"Nothing is the matter with me." Ripp's tone was clipped. Except that he was mixed-up and crazy. He should have phoned Lucita today and asked her for a date this evening. He figured by now she'd been expecting him to either call or show up at the ranch. But for some reason his heart had stubbornly refused to let him make contact with her, which didn't make sense. He ached like hell to be with her, yet at the same time he couldn't help but wonder if he was wasting his time, hanging on to a dream that might never come true. Just like the dream that his mother would one day reappear and throw her arms around him. He'd been waiting for twenty-nine years and it still hadn't happened.

Thankfully, before Mac could make any sort of reply, the waitress arrived with their meal. She placed a platter of fish in front of Ripp, then another in front of Mac.

"I had the cook rush yours, honey," she said in a syrupy voice to Mac. "Y'all want anything else?"

Mac reached out and coiled a hand around her tiny wrist. "Yeah. You goin' to the Dry Gulch after work tonight?"

She looked at his hold on her, then grinned as she lifted her gaze back to his. "I wouldn't miss it."

"What about that boyfriend of yours?" Mac asked. "He's not gonna come around and ruin things, is he?"

Ripp wanted to pick up a piece of fish and throw it right at his brother's goofy smile.

"Don't worry about him," the waitress said in a hushed voice. "I've already sent him packing."

Someone across the room began to bang a spoon against their empty coffee cup. The waitress hurried off and Ripp threw another hopeless look at his brother.

"That's just what she's going to do to you, too, Mac. Toss you away like an old dishrag when she's done with you."

Mac laughed. "Sure she will. But I'll enjoy myself on the way to the trash heap."

"I don't understand you," Ripp said with a shake of his head. "Brenna should have taught you better than to play games with women."

Mac's face went sober as he picked up his fork and stabbed it into a piece of crisp catfish. "The key word is *play,* Ripp. If a man never takes a woman seriously, he'll be just fine."

Ripp looked down at the plate of food in front of him. He needed to eat. His stomach was gnawing, but his appetite was as dead as his spirits.

"What's wrong now?" Mac asked after several moments passed. "You're not eating."

Ripp purposely lifted a bite of food to his mouth and began to chew. "I've broken your cardinal rule," he said sullenly. "And I don't know what to do about it."

Mac's brow furrowed with confusion as he turned his attention to the plate of food. "What are you talking about?"

"Getting serious about a woman," Ripp said bluntly. "I did—I have—and it hasn't worked. At least, it hasn't worked the way I wanted it to."

"Hell, it's been years since Pam walked out on you. Can't you get over that dumb female? She was a loser, Ripp. She didn't know when she had a good thing. You're better off without her."

"I'm not talking about Pam."

This brought Mac's head up and he stared in wonder at Ripp. "You mean—the Sandbur heiress? Lucita? You've fallen for her? Damn, Ripp! What were you thinking? She's not in our caliber."

"You're wrong there. Lucita isn't a snob. That isn't the problem."

Confusion wrinkled Mac's forehead. "Then what is the problem? You asked her out and she refused?"

A bitter laugh gurgled up from Ripp's throat. "Mac, if only that were the case. I can deal with being turned down for a date. This was—things got way beyond asking Lucita for a date. I asked her to marry me."

Mac was so flabbergasted that he fell back against his chair and let out a long breath. "Well, you've surprised the hell out of me, brother. I realize you've been getting close to her son, but I didn't know you'd been getting *that* close to her!"

"Yeah, well, I guess I surprised myself. I don't know what made me blurt out the marriage word to her. It was stupid. And way too soon to say it to her. But I…love her, Mac."

For once his brother appeared seriously concerned. "I take it she turned you down."

"Flatly. But she wanted us to continue on with our—relationship." Ripp wasn't about to use the word *lover* with Mac, even though his brother's mind had probably already leaped to that conclusion. "I agreed and tried to be understanding with her. But I'm miserable, Mac."

"Why?" Mac asked with obvious dismay. "Hell, be glad she isn't cutting you off completely. After a while you can change her mind about marriage."

Now that he'd released some of his pent-up feelings, Ripp realized he was hungry and he began to fork the fish up to his mouth. Between bites, he said, "I've been telling myself that exact thing, Mac. But I just feel so damned hurt. I wanted her to—" He paused, looking down at his food as he shook his head. "When I talked to her about marriage I guess I wanted her to…cling to me, to tell me she couldn't bear to be away from me for any amount of time. Because that's the way I feel about her. It didn't happen and now I feel like a fool."

Mac thoughtfully regarded Ripp's glum features. "Ripp, you can't hurry love. Or a woman. From what you've said, one man has already put her through hell. Give her time to realize you're not going to break her heart."

Break her heart! He'd told the woman that he loved her! She ought to know he'd never do anything to hurt her.

"In other words, be happy with any sort of crumbs of affection that she's willing to give me," Ripp said with frustration.

"You want to hear what I really think about all this?" Mac asked after a moment.

Ripp looked wearily across the table at his brother. "You might as well tell me. You will eventually, anyway."

"I think you're suffering from a bad case of pride."

Ripp sputtered and nearly spewed coffee across the table. "Pride?" he finally managed to choke out. "How could you say that? I don't have any pride. Pam whacked it to pieces and now Lucita has stomped those bits into the dirt. I don't know why I was stupid enough to think I'd found a woman who might actually want to make a life with me."

"Lucita isn't Pam," Mac pointed out.

"It's not just Pam. Our mother—"

"Is gone," Mac interrupted sharply. "She has nothing to do with now—with you. Unless you let her."

The next morning was Sunday. Lucita attended church with her family, then made a light lunch for herself and Marti.

Her son had been very quiet throughout the meal. Once it was over he'd gone to the living room to watch television instead of going outside to enjoy the warm afternoon as he normally would on the weekends. Lucita was very concerned about his withdrawn behavior. Right after the kidnapping had been resolved, he'd appeared to be returning to his regular self. But now he seemed to be sliding backward and she was afraid to admit that the change in him was a result of Ripp's absence.

Since that night they'd made love, Lucita had neither seen nor heard from him. Not that she'd expected him to contact her the next day, but she should have heard from him before now. She could only believe that he'd changed his mind about the two of them being together. He'd been very withdrawn after she'd explained that she couldn't marry him anytime soon. Maybe he'd decided she wasn't worth waiting for, she thought sadly. Still, she'd never imagined he would hold any of that against Marti. He'd promised her son that he would see him soon, but soon was quickly coming and going.

Sighing wearily, Lucita left the kitchen and walked out to the living room where Marti was lying on the floor, staring in a bored stupor at the television screen.

"What are you watching?"

"I don't know." He swiped a hand at the fringe of hair falling in his eyes. "Somethin' about frogs and how they help to keep insects controlled."

"Hmm. I didn't know you were that interested in science programs."

His shrug was halfhearted. "Well, there's nothin' else to watch. And I don't have anything to do outside."

Lucita eased down in a nearby armchair. "That's not true. You could invite Gracia to go horseback riding. Or we could go for a swim in the pool."

A grimace on his face, he continued to stare at the television screen. "Gracia is goin' shopping with Aunt Juliet this afternoon. And I could never talk her out of goin' 'cause she's gonna get a new pair of boots."

Smiling wanly, Lucita asked, "Is that why you're so out of sorts? You want a new pair of boots, too?"

The frown on his round face deepened. "Shoot no! I don't want that pointy-toed kind like she wants. They're girlie. Besides, I got good boots."

"Well then, I—"

Before Lucita could make another suggestion, Marti turned his head and looked at her. His expression was anxious, almost pleading and she had to fight the urge to pluck him off the floor and cradle him in her arms as though he was three years old instead of eleven.

"Mom, do you think Ripp will call soon?"

Lucita's heart hurt so badly she wondered how it could keep beating. "I don't know, son. I'm sure he's been busy."

Marti's troubled gaze dropped to the floor. "Maybe he got mad at me about somethin'," he mumbled. "Maybe I said somethin' wrong."

Rising from her seat, she squatted on her heels and rubbed a hand over her son's thick hair. "Oh, Marti, of course Ripp didn't get mad at you. He likes you a whole lot. I'm sure of that. And I—"

The ring of the telephone interrupted her words and for a moment she almost ignored it in order to finish what she considered a very important conversation with her son. But the ringing continued, intruding on the moment.

Sighing, she rose to her feet and walked over to an end table where a portable phone was sitting in its cradle.

Not bothering to look at the caller identification, she snatched it up and quickly answered, "Sanchez residence."

"Lucita, it's Ripp."

The sound of his voice was both sweet and painful. She gripped the phone and tried to continue breathing in a normal way. But her heart had already jumped into overdrive and her knees began to quiver.

"Hello," she replied. "How are you?"

"Great. Just great," he said in an almost-cheery voice. "Is Marti there? I want to apologize to him for not calling sooner. I've been—tied up with work."

And trying to avoid her, Lucita wondered. Perhaps he'd read her plea to take things slowly as a sign that she didn't need to be close to him. How could she explain that her trust in men had been broken? She was terrified to even think of being a wife again, yet she very much wanted his love.

"Yes, he's here. Would you like to speak with him?" she asked, keeping her voice as casual as possible.

"Yes. But I want to ask you something first."

If possible, her grip on the phone tightened until her knuckles began to ache under the pressure. "All right. What is it?"

"I'd like to invite Marti over to my place for the afternoon. Is that okay with you?"

"Of course."

There was a long, tense pause as she waited and hoped in the next moment he would invite her to join them. Instead he said, "Good. I thought it would be nice for the two of us to spend some time together. Just a male thing—you understand?"

Clearly. He was pointedly distancing himself from her. But why? He'd told her that he loved her. Had that all been a lie? Her throat was suddenly so tight that when she replied, it felt as though the words were ripping away part of her vocal cords. "Sure. I understand. And it will be good for Marti. I'll put him on the phone."

She walked over to Marti and with a smile she was far from feeling handed the phone down to him. "Here's a person I think you'll want to talk to."

The minute her son heard Ripp's voice, his face started shining like the sun bursting over the Sandbur on a spring morning. Nothing that she'd been able to do or say this past week had made him happy. Now one call from Ripp had him jumping to his feet and grinning like a mischievous elf.

Not waiting to hear Marti's side of the conversation, Lucita slipped out of the room and wiped at the tears burning her eyes.

Later that evening, just before dark, Lucita finished her lesson plans for the coming school week and started wandering restlessly through the house, trying to keep her mind busy and direct it away from Ripp and Marti. Each passing minute in the empty house was only making it worse.

Finally, she decided to walk over to the big house to see if Juliet and Gracia were back from their shopping excursion. As she was going through the kitchen on her way out, she heard a truck pull to a stop in front of the house. If it was Ripp bringing Marti home, would he come in and speak to her?

Pausing in her tracks, she held her breath, waiting for the sound of footsteps while asking herself what she could possibly say to the man. That she still wanted them to be lovers?

Rolling her eyes with helpless despair, she thrust a hand through her tousled hair. Clearly that idea hadn't pleased him. So where did that leave her? With empty, aching arms and a troubled mind, she told herself.

After a moment, she heard the door at the front of the house open and close and then her son's footsteps running through the living room. No other sounds followed. It was painfully obvious to Lucita, even before she heard the engine of his truck fire back to life, that Ripp wasn't coming in to see her. He didn't *want* to see her.

"Mom? Mom! Where are you?"

Drawing in a bracing breath, she turned away from the door and headed toward the sound of her son.

Feigning a cheery expression, she called to him, "In the kitchen."

In a matter of seconds Marti raced into the room, then skidded to a stop on the tiled floor. His face was a glow of smiles, a complete contradiction to the child she'd seen earlier this morning.

"Gee, Mom, why is it so dark in here?"

Surprised that she hadn't noticed the shadows filling up the house, she looked around her. "Oh, I was about to go over to the big house to see if Juliet and Gracia have come home. I—uh—didn't want to leave any unnecessary lights burning."

Seeming to accept her reasoning, he said, "Well, Gracia and Aunt Juliet ain't back yet. So come here and sit down. I wanta tell you everything that me and Ripp did at his place. You wanta hear about it, don't you?"

He was so excited the words were tumbling from him like an auctioneer with a bidding war on his hands.

"Yes, I want to hear. Just quit saying *ain't,* though, or I'm going to make you write it until you'll wish you'd never heard the word before."

Laughing at her threat, he tugged her over to the table. Feeling as though she'd just switched roles and was now the child, she sat in one of the chairs and after folding her hands in her lap, gave Marti her full attention.

"Okay," she said, "First of all, did you have a good time?"

Of course the question was unneeded. It was quite evident that Marti was on top of the world. But she was going through all the motions for her son's sake. Spending time with Ripp was important to him and she had to accept that, even if the man had left an ache in her heart.

"It was super, Mom. Just super. Ripp has a really neat place! And he has this dog named Chester. He's black and he's so smart you just wouldn't believe it. I think he understands human talk."

Lucita had never mentioned to Marti that she'd visited Ripp's home the weekend before. If things had ended on a happy note between the two of them, she would have loved telling Marti about Chester, Ripp's carpentry work, his garden and all the other things she'd seen. But after their tepid parting that night, she'd decided it was best to keep her visit bottled inside with the rest of her memories.

"Did you like Chester?"

"Boy, did I! We wrestled and played fetch and all that kind of stuff. He ain—isn't like the curs here on the ranch. He likes to have fun."

Lucita smiled. "The curs are working dogs. They're too tired from running cattle to want to race around and play."

Marti's freckled nose wrinkled up as he considered his mother's comment. "Yeah, I guess you're right. Chester's just a pet and the curs are cowhands."

Glad her son could respect the difference, she reached over and ruffled the top of his hair. "Are you hungry? There's leftover spaghetti in the fridge."

Marti rubbed his tummy. "I already had supper with Ripp. He fixed smoked sausage on the grill and we ate it on bread with mustard. And we ate ice cream right out of the container. He says that's the way a real man eats ice cream. Did you know that, Mom?"

The only thing Lucita knew was that there were hot tears pouring down the sides of her heart, scalding it with pain. All she'd ever wanted was a family of her own, to know that she and her child were loved and wanted. Ultimately, Derek hadn't cared about anyone but himself. His desertion and betrayal had torn deep wounds into both Lucita and Marti.

Yet now, as she watched the animated joy on her son's face as he talked about Ripp, she realized that her son was brave enough to move on, to accept love where it was offered. She wasn't that brave. And it was killing her.

"No. I didn't know men had a special way of eating ice cream," she said, pushing the words through her aching throat. "So what else did you and Ripp do, besides eat?"

"We went fishin' in the pond! With cane poles—like people used to do way back in the olden days. The poles had corks and hooks and we had to dig worms in the garden to use for bait. Ripp says that sun perch love grub worms, so we found as many of them as we could."

Smiling as best she could, Lucita asked, "Did you catch any?"

"Shoot yeah! I caught eight! Ripp cleaned them and put them in the freezer. He says we'll cook 'em and eat 'em the next time I come to visit."

So Ripp was planning to have a next time with Marti. She thanked God that he wasn't going to let his differences with her stand in the way of his relationship with her son. Even if he didn't understand her feelings, he seemed to recognize that Marti needed him. And she loved him for that.

Yes, she still loved him. The realization was something she was going to have to get used to, she told herself. Because she couldn't see her heart changing or forgetting.

"Ripp has a brother and he's a deputy, too. His name

is Mac and Ripp says Mac has a boat—a big one. And that one of these days we'll take it to the ocean and fish in the saltwater!" Marti tilted his head thoughtfully from side to side. "Wouldn't that be somethin'? To have a brother who did the same thing as you? I think that would be neat. Really neat. Don't you, Mom?"

Did Marti wish for a brother? Of course, he did. In the past, he'd often asked for a sibling. And for a long time, Lucita had promised to give him one. Yet the right time to get pregnant again had never seemed to come. And then her marriage had come to an abrupt end. Her plans, her hopes and dreams had all come crashing down. But that didn't mean her life had ended. Did it?

"Well, I have two brothers," she replied. "But I can't see Matt or Cordero teaching geometry."

That idea tickled Marti enormously and he giggled outright. "Uncle Matt would probably wear his chaps and spurs in the classroom and Uncle Cordero would have the students dancing and singing instead of working on math."

"I think you have a clear picture of your uncles," Lucita said with wry amusement.

His face suddenly sobering, Marti rose from the chair to stand at the edge of the table, closer to his mother. "Mom, this is—I'm gonna say somethin' that's probably stupid. But I'm gonna say it anyway."

Caught by the sudden change in him, Lucita stared at the mixture of emotions parading across his boyish features. Happiness. Sadness. Confusion. Hope. It was as if she was seeing everything in her heart mirrored on her son's face.

"You know that Faye Warner woman—she was creepy and she stunk like cigarettes and beer and I wasn't sure if she'd hurt me or not. She said she wouldn't hurt me, but she was a bad person and I figured she was lying. But I—now after everything is over with, I'm almost glad that she took me."

Stunned now, Lucita's eyes flew wide-open. "Marti!" she gasped. "Why? That doesn't make sense? Were you angry with me or someone else here on the ranch and you wanted to get away? I don't understand."

One corner of his mouth dipped downward. "See, I told you it was gonna sound crazy. But if she hadn't took me then Ripp wouldn't have come looking for me. And I wouldn't have him for a buddy now."

Overwhelmed by her son's admission, she reached over and rubbed a hand gently over Marti's forearm. "You met Ripp before Faye Warner grabbed you at the rodeo. You didn't act like you even liked him then."

His gaze dropped guiltily to the floor as he shrugged both shoulders. "That was before I knew that Dad was dead—and that he'd done all those bad things." He lifted his head to meet his mother's troubled gaze. "Now I can see that Ripp—well, he could never be a bad person like Dad was. He won't ever leave me. 'Cause he ain't like that. I just know it."

He won't ever leave me.

Her son was willing to trust again. Love again. Why couldn't she?

She was aching, wondering, trying to picture the future when Marti slapped a hand over his mouth in sudden dawning.

"Uh-oh, sorry, Mom. I forgot and said *ain't*."

Laughing through her tears, she reached to hug him to her. "This time I forgive you, son."

Chapter Twelve

The next evening, in a room at the back of the sheriff's department, Ripp sat on the edge of a metal chair while Officer Tava Hollis wound a bandage around his upper arm.

Only an hour earlier Ripp and the sheriff had responded to a domestic incidence on the south side of town. While the two of them listened to the woman's version of the confrontation, Ripp had glanced around just in time to see the male offender armed with a butcher knife, running straight for the sheriff's back.

Ripp hadn't hesitated or even taken one split second to react. He'd lunged between the sheriff and the offender and wrestled the knife from his hand. But not before Ripp's arm had taken a deep stab from the kitchen utensil.

"This needs stitches, Ripp," the young woman exclaimed with a frown. "Before you head home, you'd better go by the emergency room and let a doctor deal with this."

Ripp grunted. "It's just a scratch and it hasn't been that long ago since I got a tetanus shot. I'll live."

Tava clicked her tongue with disapproval. "A knife blade slicing into your bicep is not a minor scratch, Ripp. What happened anyway? Sheriff Travers didn't say, except that you saved his life."

Ripp released a mocking snort as she finished taping down one end of the thick gauze. "I was just doing my job. There wasn't anything heroic about it. In fact, I should have noticed that the guy had slipped back inside. Any bastard that would beat his wife can't be trusted."

Grinning, the blond officer jerked her head toward the lockup area situated at the very back of the building. "He's raising hell in his cell right now. Swearing he hasn't done anything to warrant being jailed."

Ripp let out a weary breath. Normally he felt good after he'd put a jerk like Ron Whitman behind bars. Society was safer. Women were safer. But this evening he only felt a weary defeatism that was totally out of character for him.

Hell, who was he kidding. Ever since Lucita had turned down his marriage proposal, he'd felt utterly defeated. He'd felt lost and hurt. The same way he'd felt when his mother had walked out of the house with a pair of suitcases in her hands.

"Let him tell his story in court," Ripp replied. "I can't wait to testify and put the creep away for a long time."

"There." Tava patted the last piece of adhesive tape

in place then stepped back to admire her handiwork. "That will fix you up until you can see a doctor."

Rising from the chair, he strode to the door to exit the room. "Thanks, Tava. I'll do that tomorrow—sometime."

As he walked down the hallway to the sheriff's office, Ripp could hear Tava yelling warnings at him about the cut getting infected. She meant well, but at the moment, Ripp could care less about the aching wound in his arm. The pain in his heart was much worse.

After a light rap against the sheriff's door, Ripp stuck his head inside the small, messy office. His boss was on the telephone, but once he noticed Ripp, he made a motioning gesture with his hand for him to enter the room.

Ripp stepped inside and took a seat in one of the folding metal chairs in front of the desk while he waited for the other man to finish his conversation.

Once Travers hung up the phone, he looked pointedly at Ripp. "On your way home?"

Ripp nodded. "Yeah. Unless you need me for something else. I'm pretty beat."

The sheriff's gaze zeroed in on Ripp's arm. "Better have a doc look at that. You lost a lot of blood. And even if I thanked you before, I'm saying it again. You had my back, buddy. Literally. I won't ever forget that."

Ripp batted a dismissive hand through the air. "Forget it. You'd do the same if the situation had been reversed. It's just a part of this crazy job we have."

Rye Travers leaned back in his chair and studied Ripp with a narrowed gaze. "Speaking of this job, Ripp, I was planning on talking with you before we got the domestic call. Has something happened here at work to upset you? I haven't noticed any tension with the other deputies, but—"

"No. All the guys are great," he cut in. "I'm fine. Everything is fine."

The other man frowned. "I hate to call a man a liar, Ripp. But I can usually tell when someone isn't telling me the truth. You're holding something back."

A tight grimace on his face, Ripp pulled off his Stetson and raked a hand through his hair. "Okay. I'm—uh—having a few personal problems."

"Oh." The other lawman picked up a pen and tapped it thoughtfully against the ink blotter on his desk. "I hope you and Mac aren't out of sorts with each other. You two are the only family you have to speak of. You need to stick together."

"We do. Always. I irritate him and he annoys me, but we love each other. That could never change."

The sheriff smiled. "Good. I'm glad to hear it. I just want to make sure all my deputies are in a good state of mind. And happy, if that's possible."

How long had it been since he'd actually been happy? Ripp wondered. For years now, especially after Pam had walked out on him, he'd settled for just having a normal life, not necessarily a happy one. Yet he hadn't realized exactly what he'd been missing out on until Lucita had come into his life. Loving her had made him question every choice he'd ever made for his future.

Propping his ankle upon his knee, Ripp leaned forward. "Rye, do you ever remember Dad talking about his wife—my mother?"

Rye's dark brows lifted with surprise. "That's not something I remember your dad doing much—talking about his personal life. But there were a few times."

"And?"

The sheriff's eyes narrowed shrewdly on Ripp's face. "Why are you asking about your mother now? You never have before."

Ripp looked away from the sheriff and stared unseeingly at a large map of Texas pinned to the office wall. Right now the misery in his heart felt that massive.

Biting back a sigh, he said, "Maybe because I didn't think it was that important before. But I've been thinking about things here lately. Marti Sanchez—his father deserted him and Lucita. Just seeing the shadows in that little boy's eyes reminded me of when Mom left. Mac and I didn't understand. We thought she'd skipped out because of us."

Rye's expression was suddenly pensive. "The Sanchez kid—I guess all of us guys imagined ourselves at his age, going through what he did with that crazy woman. And having to face the fact that his father died a criminal."

"Well, Marti has a good mother to make up for all that," Ripp said, then glanced around to see a thoughtful frown furrowing his friend's brow.

"Yeah, some of us are lucky like that, Ripp. As for your mother, I can't really tell you much about what went on between your parents. Didn't you ever talk to your dad about Frankie?"

Ripp shook his head. All he could remember about his mother was a woman with long black hair and shoulders slumped in weariness. She'd seemed tired all the time and her blue eyes, eyes the same color as his own, had held no light or hope. Looking back on it now, Ripp realized she must have been very unhappy. But why? Because she was tired of the responsibility of caring for two rambunctious sons? Tired of living on a farm where hard work was always waiting to be done?

"No," Ripp said quietly. "That subject was taboo. Mac and I understood that if we mentioned her, we'd have a cold door shut in our face. So we didn't. Mom's parents lived in California, so they were out of the picture, Dad was the one who was there, showing us love and guidance, giving us food and shelter and anything else we needed. It seemed almost hateful to hurt him in that way. So we kept our mouths shut about her."

Rye nodded. "Well, Owen didn't mention Frankie often and when he did it was usually with bitterness. But the last time he brought her name up, it was on one Mother's Day. She'd called him, he'd said, on the first Mother's Day after she'd left the farm. I'm really not sure why Owen brought the matter up in the first place. I certainly didn't. All I can figure is that the memory was hounding him and he needed to talk about it."

His mind spinning, Ripp stared expectantly at him. "What else did he say? Anything?"

The other man suddenly grimaced, as though he wasn't certain he should have opened his mouth at all. "You haven't heard any of this before?"

"No. This is all news to me."

Wiping a hand over his face, the sheriff said, "If Owen were still alive I wouldn't be betraying his confidence. But he's gone and I can see you need to hear this." Shifting forward in his seat, he leveled his gaze on Ripp. "Owen told me that Frankie called begging to come home. Said she'd realized she'd made a mistake. She wanted to be with you boys, but Owen refused to let her anywhere near you and Mac or even himself. He didn't trust her. He didn't want to give her the chance to hurt the three of you all over again. Maybe he did the right thing. Or maybe he missed the chance to have his family back together again. I think your dad probably went to his grave wondering if he'd made the right decision."

His mother had called! His mother had *wanted* to come home. Down through the years Owen had let his sons believe that she'd turned away from them completely and never once looked back. Now Ripp had to face the fact that there had been two sides to the story, details that their dad had purposely kept from them.

Strangled with emotions, Ripp looked at the floor and slowly turned his head from one side to the other. "Of all the things I expected to hear—it wasn't this. He never told us. He let us think—"

Across the desk, he could hear his longtime friend sigh with regret.

"Ripp, your dad wasn't some god with a shiny badge pinned to his chest. He was just a man, a very human man. And sometimes we men make mistakes. He loved you. Be grateful for that."

We men make mistakes. The words rang through Ripp like a clanging bell and the reverberation couldn't be ignored. Rye was right about men making mistakes. Ripp had made a big one with Lucita. He'd expected too much from her too soon. He'd let his wounded pride blind every ounce of common sense he possessed.

Rising to his feet, he pulled on his Stetson and started to the door. "I can forgive him, Rye. 'Cause I've made a big mistake myself," he said grimly.

As Ripp reached for the door handle to let himself out, Rye said, "Most mistakes are fixable. I'll bet this one isn't as big as you think."

"I don't know," Ripp muttered. "But I'm about to find out."

* * *

Lucita's hands were trembling as she parked the old ranch truck at the side of the sheriff's department building and reached for the door handle.

She didn't know why she was getting so nervous about her decision to face Ripp. For all she knew, he might have already headed home for the evening. And even if he was still on duty, he might be busy with paperwork, or on patrol.

Of course, she still had his cell number. But she'd been too cowardly to call it, too afraid that he wouldn't give her a chance to say anything personal between them.

And if you do find him here, what are you going to say now, Lucitá? That you've been an idiot? That you didn't realize just how much you loved him until he was out of your life? Dear God, that sounded so lame, so silly. She wouldn't blame him if he refused to forgive her. But she had to try. Marti had opened her eyes. He'd made her see that if she couldn't trust, she might as well give up everything meaningful in life. Would Ripp understand that?

Her high heels felt as if they were made of lead as she walked into the building and over to the waist-high counter where the same female officer with a blond ponytail was sitting at the small desk. Throughout the ordeal with Marti's kidnapping, Lucita had learned her name was Tava and that she'd left her studies at Sul Ross University to embark on a career in law enforcement.

Tonight, recognition crossed the young woman's face as she spotted Lucita at the counter. Smiling, she rose to her feet. "Hello, Ms. Sanchez. How can I help you this evening? I hope you haven't had more trouble."

Feeling a blush sting her cheeks, Lucita quickly shook her head. "No. Don't worry. Everything is finally quiet and peaceful on the ranch. Uh—I was—" Nervously, she swallowed and tried to start again. "Actually, I stopped by to see if Deputy McCleod was around. I—"

"I'm right here."

The sound of Ripp's low voice momentarily stunned her motionless. And then a mixture of dread and eagerness sent her heart into a rapid thud as she slowly turned to see he was standing only a few feet behind her.

"Ripp."

It was all she could say and somewhere in the back of her mind, Lucita realized that behind them Tava was probably wondering what was going on, why the small foyer was suddenly charged with undercurrents.

"Is something wrong? Has something happened?" he asked.

Weeks ago she'd stood in this same spot and he'd asked her the same question, she realized. After finding the note pinned to her truck, she'd been terrified and she'd run straight to this man. Even then, something inside her had trusted him, but somewhere along the way, her head had gotten in the way of her heart. The night they'd made love she should have told him how she really felt. Now she could only hope it wasn't too late.

"Uh—no. Nothing has happened." His blue eyes were riveted on her face and she felt her heart jerk into an even faster gear as she met his questioning gaze. "I…was just on my way home from work and I…stopped by to see if…I could… If you have time to talk."

She was sounding more stupid by the minute, she realized, as her gaze slipped from his face. Then she noticed the crude bandage wrapped around his upper arm. Moments ago, when she turned to see him, she'd been too shaken to notice it. Now she couldn't stop herself from rushing forward and planting her hands against his chest.

"Ripp! Your arm! What happened?"

Not bothering to answer, he grabbed her by the forearm and marched her through the double doors that were the exit to the building. Outside, dusk had fallen and most of the parking slots around the municipal compound were now empty. Across the way, street-lamps were beginning to flicker to life and closer, on the manicured lawn, a pair of mourning doves were deciding it was time to roost.

Lucita's mind whirled as he guided her to the side of the building, out of sight of anyone who entered or exited the front. What was he thinking? Was seeing her again tilting his world the same way that the touch of his hand was shaking hers?

Eventually, he stopped their forward motion and turned to her. As Lucita looked up at him, she realized that just seeing his rugged face was like a warm rain after a cold, dry winter and she soaked up the precious sight.

"The arm is nothing," he explained. "Just a little run-in with a butcher knife. What I want to know is what are you doing here?"

He didn't sound angry. Nor did he sound pleased, she decided as she carefully studied the guarded expression on his face. Sucking in a bracing breath, she tried to make sense as she answered, "I—I'm sorry I just showed up like this, Ripp. I realize I should have called. But I wanted to speak with you in person. To tell you…that I was wrong. The other night at your place—I said all the wrong things to you and I—I'm sorry."

As she waited for him to respond, she could feel herself breathing hard, as though she was waiting to hear a verdict of life or death.

Aeons seemed to pass as he quietly studied her face and then to her utter surprise he tilted his head back and laughed toward the tree limbs above their heads.

"Oh, Lucita! This is incredible and you're probably not going to believe me, but—"

He looked back down at her and this time she could see the soft light of love in his eyes. Even before he spoke another word, her heart soared with hope.

"But what?" she prompted.

"Before you walked in I had already decided to call you tonight. I didn't know how I was going to do it, but I knew I had to change your mind about marrying me."

She opened her mouth to speak, but he quickly shook his head to stop her.

"No. Just let me say this, Lucita. You said you were wrong. Well, I was even more wrong. Damn, I—this past week or so has been—I've walked around like a dead man. Just tell me what you want of me, Lucita. I'll give it to you. Time. Patience. I'll do anything. Just give me a chance to become your husband."

Feeling as though the world had just settled back on its axis, Lucita smiled up at him. "What I want from you isn't complicated, my darling. All you have to do is be my husband and love me forever."

He closed his eyes and beneath her palms she could feel a rush of air leave his lungs, his heart pounding wildly in his chest.

"Come on," he muttered thickly. "We're going home."

Fifteen minutes later they were in Ripp's bedroom. He'd not taken the time to turn on even one light, so the house was dark. The only sounds to be heard were the whisper of clothing against skin as garments slid to the floor, gasps of pleasure as lips and hands touched and worshipped, soft words carried on notes of raw emotion.

Their bodies came together quickly, without the need for more questions or answers. It was enough for Lucita to know that Ripp loved her and wanted her. The rest would take care of itself.

When their spiraling climb to rapture finally descended back to earth, Lucita once again found her head pillowed on Ripp's shoulder. Only this time there were no doubts lingering in her mind. No wall guarding her heart.

As she glided a hand across his hard abdomen she was filled with a sense of peace and homecoming.

"Tell me, Lucita, what made you change your mind? When I saw you at the sheriff's office I was shocked. I'd convinced myself that you didn't really care for me at all."

The corners of her mouth lifted lazily upward as she drew tiny circles upon his damp skin. "Marti convinced me. He loves you. He trusts you. He made me see that if I couldn't trust you, too, I'd lose any chance at happiness."

Tilting her head slightly, she studied his face. His eyes were closed and a day-old growth of whiskers covered his jaws. There was a haggard edge to his features, yet in spite of that she could see a sense of contented relief. Knowing that she'd given him that much swelled her heart.

One of his hands stroked the back of her head, down the long length of her hair, then onto the bare skin below. "I don't know how you can forgive me, Lucita. I've behaved like a selfish ass. All I was thinking about was myself. When you turned down my marriage proposal all I could think was that you were just like the other two women in my life that I'd tried to love. First my mother left, then Pam. And there you were saying you weren't ready to make a life with me. I felt so rejected. I wasn't thinking about all that you'd been through with Derek, or that you might have been afraid to jump into marriage again."

"I was afraid," she agreed.

His head shook against the pillow. "Mac told me my pride was getting in my way. I didn't want to believe that he could be right. Until tonight, after something Sheriff Travers told me."

Very curious now, Lucita raised up on her elbow to look at him. "Really? What could he have said that pertained to us?"

"I learned something about my parents." His eyes connected with hers. "You see, my mother left when Mac and I were something like eight and ten years old. Dad didn't tell us, but we heard through the local gossip chain that she'd run off with some guy who operated a tire business in town. At that age we didn't much understand the connotation of what that 'other man' meant. We only knew she'd left us boys behind and that she must have really hated us."

"Oh, Ripp. Just like Marti. That's so awful. Didn't your father explain what happened? Later, when you were old enough to understand?"

"He wouldn't talk about her. Except to say 'the damn

woman was sorry, that's all' or 'she didn't deserve the home I tried to give her.' Mac and I pretty much agreed with Dad. Especially as time went by and she never showed her face again."

Aching for him, Lucita gently stroked her fingertips against his temple. "So you never heard from her again?"

"No. And until tonight I'd believed that she'd turned her back on us completely. The sheriff told me that shortly after she left our farm, she called my father and told him that she'd made a bad mistake. She wanted to come home and be a family with us again. But Dad refused to let her return. Guess he couldn't trust her. Or maybe by then he didn't love her anymore. All I know is that she didn't hate us boys. She wanted to be our mother. But Dad kept her out of our lives and led us to believe that's the way she wanted things."

"She could have fought him," Lucita pointed out.

"Yeah. But you didn't know Owen McCleod. He was like a piece of unbending iron. I guess she decided she was too weak to fight him. Especially after her tryst with the tire man. She must have thought the whole town viewed her as a jezebel."

Piqued by his sad tale, Lucita leaned over and switched on a small lamp at the head of the bed. Once the soft orb of light shed a golden hue over his face, she said, "I don't believe that, Ripp."

A faint frown marred his forehead. "What do you mean by that?"

"I mean that your mother didn't sound like the sort of woman who'd simply give up what she wanted. Something else must have happened to her."

"Are you thinking that she might have died?" Ripp asked.

Lucita nodded. "Maybe. Or perhaps some person or thing stood in her way. Have you ever tried to contact her?"

"No. Never wanted to. I could only see the misery she caused. Now, well… I'm going to think about searching." The seriousness on his face suddenly disappeared and with a wicked grin, he pulled her head down to his. "That's enough about the past. Tonight is all about you and me—us."

He nibbled a soft kiss on her lips, but before he could deepen the embrace, Lucita pulled her head back and rubbed the tip of her nose to his.

"And tonight I want to make sure that you know how much I love you, Ripp. How much I will *always* love you."

A wondrous light glinted in his blue eyes. "Always? That sounds like a forever kind of thing."

"It is a forever kind of thing. I want to be your wife. That is," she added provocatively, "if you still want me."

His hands went still against her back. "Wife." He repeated the word as though it was the most precious sound he'd ever heard. "Lucita, I thought you needed more time. If you do—"

His words halted as she began to shake her head. "Time is the last thing I need. I had a week and two days to think, Ripp, and that's all the time I needed to show me what I was doing—running scared, hiding in the past, worrying about the future instead of living it. In the end I was mainly wasting precious days that we could be together. I don't want to waste any more. Do you?"

Drawing her head back down to his, he whispered against her lips, "No, my love. Our life together—it'll never be wasted."

Three months later on a quiet Sunday evening, Lucita stood at a front window of her new home and gazed at the limbs of the Chinese Pistache trees drooping below the eave of the porch roof. Thanksgiving had come and gone and now that Christmas was approaching, the leaves would soon turn a deep scarlet and eventually scatter beneath the cold north wind.

But before that happened the yard would be a glorious blaze of color and she was looking forward to adding even more beauty with strings of Christmas lights edging the roof and a Nativity scene out on the lawn, complete with a manger that Ripp had made himself.

"You're lost in thought. Thinking this old house needs more space?"

Glancing over her shoulder, she smiled as Ripp walked up behind her and slid his arms around her waist.

"No. I like this house just the way it is, thank you, sir."

Turning in his arms she pecked a kiss on her husband's cheek, then pointed to another spot on the living room floor. "What do you think about putting the Christmas tree there? The lights will shine through the window."

Loving her excitement over the holidays, Ripp grinned indulgently. "I suppose it's essential for the lights to be seen from the driveway?"

"Of course! Santa needs a guide to the house! How else will he know where to put our gifts?"

"Who says you're going to get any gifts?" he teased.

She wrinkled her nose impishly at him. "Well, you are. I've already got something very special picked out. In fact—" She grabbed his hand, led him out of the living room and down a short hallway until they reached their bedroom. "Since I've asked you about where to put the Christmas tree, maybe you can advise me about this."

Pulling away from him, she went to a corner of the room that wasn't already taken up with furniture and spread out her arms as though she was measuring space.

"Do you think a crib will fit here? I think it would be a perfect spot. Not too far away from our bed, but not too close, either."

When he didn't say anything, she looked around to see he was completely bemused.

"A what?" he finally uttered.

Walking back to him, she took up his hands with hers and squeezed his fingers. "A crib," she repeated with a patient and very loving smile. "For the baby. Our baby."

"Baby," he whispered with awe. "Are you sure?"

Her face glowing, she nodded. "Nicci gave me a very accurate test. I used it this morning after we came home from church. But I didn't really need it to tell me that I was carrying your child. I could already feel the change in me."

As Lucita's announcement sunk in, he tugged her into his arms and held her so tightly that her cheek was smashed against his chest.

"Oh, Lucita, you can't imagine how happy you've made me. Or how much I love you."

Tears of joy glazed her eyes and spiked her lashes. "I suspect it's about as much as I love you," she murmured.

Eventually, he eased his hold on her enough to look

down at her face. "What about Marti? How is he going to take this news? I want him to be happy, too."

She chuckled at the thought of the joyful reaction they were going to get from Marti when they told him about the coming baby.

"As soon as Marti comes home we'll tell him together. He's going to be thrilled to have a sibling. And I have a sneaking suspicion that he's going to want more than one brother or sister."

"We can handle that," Ripp said with a sexy chuckle.

"Okay, big guy, can you handle this? I want something special for Christmas. Something only you can give me."

His brows lifted with wry speculation. "If it's within my power. I can't make it snow for you in sixty-degree weather, though."

She playfully poked a finger in his ribs. "I want you to build a cradle for the baby. One with tiny carved spokes and runners to rock back and forth on. Can you do that for me?"

Hugging her to him, he pressed his cheek against the top of her head. "Honey, it'll be my greatest pleasure to build you a crib and love you and our children for the rest of our lives."

* * * * *

Don't miss the next title in this series
HITCHED TO THE HORSEMAN
available September 2008!

*Ladies, start your engines with a sneak preview
of Harlequin's officially licensed
NASCAR® romance series.*

Life in a famous racing family comes at a price

All his life Larry Grosso has lived in the shadow of
his well-known racing family—but it's now time
for him to take what he wants. And on top of that
list is Crystal Hayes—breathtaking, sweet…and
twenty-two years younger. But their age difference
is creating animosity within their families, and
suddenly their romance is the talk of the entire
NASCAR circuit!

*Turn the page for a sneak preview of
OVERHEATED
by Barbara Dunlop
On sale July 29 wherever books are sold.*

Rufus, as Crystal Hayes had decided to call the black Lab, slept soundly on the soft seat even as she maneuvered the Softco truck in front of the Dean Grosso garage. Engines fired through the open bay doors, compressors clacked and impact tools whined as the teams tweaked their race cars in preparation for qualifying at the third race in Charlotte.

As always when she visited the garage area, Crystal experienced a vicarious thrill, watching the technicians' meticulous, last-minute preparations. As the daughter of a machinist, she understood the difference a fraction of a degree or a thousandth of an inch could make in the performance of a race car.

She muscled the driver's door shut behind her and waved hello to a couple of familiar crew members in their white-and-pale-blue jumpsuits. Then she rounded the back of the truck and rolled up the door. Inside, five boxes were marked Cargill Motors.

One of them was big and heavy, and it had slid forward a few feet, probably when she'd braked to make the narrow parking lot entrance. So she pushed up the sleeves of her canary-yellow T-shirt, then stretched forward to reach the box. A couple of catcalls came her way as her faded blue jeans tightened across her rear end. But she knew they were good-natured, and she simply ignored them.

She dragged the box toward her over the gritty metal floor.

"Let me give you a hand with that," a deep, melodious voice rumbled in her ear.

"I can manage," she responded crisply, not wanting to engage with any of the catcallers.

Here in the garage, the last thing she needed was one of the guys treating her as if she was something other than, well, one of the guys.

She'd learned long ago there was something about her that made men toss out pickup lines like parade candy. And she'd been around race crews long enough to know she needed to behave like a buddy, not a potential date.

She piled the smaller boxes on top of the large one.

"It looks heavy," said the voice.

"I'm tough," she assured him as she scooped the pile into her arms.

He didn't move away, so she turned her head to subject him to a *back off* stare. But she found herself staring into a compelling pair of green...no, brown...no, hazel eyes. She did a double take as they seemed to twinkle, multicolored, under the garage lights.

The man insistently held out his hands for the boxes. There was a dignity in his tone and little crinkles around his eyes that hinted at wisdom. There wasn't a single sign of flirtation in his expression, but Crystal was still cautious.

"You know I'm being paid to move this, right?" she asked him.

"That doesn't mean I can't be a gentleman."

Somebody whistled from a workbench. "Go, Professor Larry."

The man named Larry tossed a "Back off" over his shoulder. Then he turned to Crystal. "Sorry about that."

"Are you for real?" she asked, growing uncomfortable with the attention they were drawing. The last thing she needed was some latter-day Sir Galahad defending her honor at the track.

He quirked a dark eyebrow in a question.

"I mean," she elaborated, "you don't need to worry. I've been fending off the wolves since I was seventeen."

"Doesn't make it right," he countered, attempting to lift the boxes from her hands.

She jerked back. "You're not making it any easier."

He frowned.

"You carry this box, and they start thinking of me as a girl."

Professor Larry dipped his gaze to take in the curves of her figure. "Hate to tell you this," he said, a little twinkle coming into those multifaceted eyes.

Something about his look made her shiver inside. It was a ridiculous reaction. Guys had given her the once-over a million times. She'd learned long ago to ignore it.

"Odds are," Larry continued, a teasing drawl in his tone, "they already have."

She turned pointedly away, boxes in hand as she marched across the floor. She could feel him watching her from behind.

* * * * *

*Crystal Hayes could do without her looks,
men obsessed with her looks, and guys who think
they're God's gift to the ladies.
Would Larry be the one guy who could blow all
of Crystal's preconceptions away?
Look for OVERHEATED
by Barbara Dunlop.
On sale July 29, 2008.*

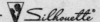

SPECIAL EDITION

A late-night walk on the beach resulted
in Trevor Marlowe's heroic rescue of a
drowning woman. He took the amnesia
victim in and dubbed her Venus, for the
goddess who'd emerged from the sea.
It looked as if she might be his goddess of
love, too...until her former fiancé showed
up on Trevor's doorstep.

Don't miss

THE BRIDE WITH NO NAME

by *USA TODAY* bestselling author
MARIE FERRARELLA

*Available August
wherever you buy books.*

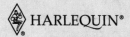

REQUEST YOUR FREE BOOKS!

2 FREE NOVELS PLUS 2 FREE GIFTS!

Silhouette®

SPECIAL EDITION®

Life, Love and Family!

COMING NEXT MONTH